A *Dark* Subconscious Journey of
Reawakening and **Power**

Simon Edwards
Door808.com

Copyright © Simon Edwards 2025

All rights reserved.

ISBN: 978-1-0369-3167-4

Artwork by Tom J Davis

No part of this work may be reproduced, stored, or transmitted in any form or by any means without prior written permission from the author.

This is a work of fiction. Any resemblance to actual persons, living or dead, or to actual events, is purely coincidental.

A catalogue record for this book is available from the British Library.

If you'd like to reach out to me or learn more about Door 808 and its characters, please visit Door808.com.

No AI has been used to create this novel.

Thank you for your support.

To Jasp,

Thank you for your support! See you on the other side of DOOR 808.

G. Edles

Author's Notes

Throughout our lives, we go through different versions of ourselves. Sometimes you can feel your younger, more eager self surfacing when something nostalgic or exciting happens. Maybe the person you were ten years ago unexpectedly comes alive when you see an old friend. It's almost as if those people you once were are still there, but... somewhere else. *Door 808* explores this idea deeply while delving into the tragic tale of Alexander Lowe, a brilliant and popular biochemist who learns to bend the laws of reality.

The idea of writing *Door 808* was very daunting when I first started putting the story together just over ten years ago. I had wanted to get my imagination down onto paper for a very long time but I had no experience and two regretful Ds in GCSE English to my name. This really discouraged me early on, and made me feel like a fraud for even considering it as a serious possibility. From 2013 to 2023, I rewrote the first half of the story a dozen times, refining my style and figuring it all out at my own pace. In 2023 I finally felt like I was ready, so I went for it and after two years of persistence I can proudly say I've finished the story I've wanted to tell for *so* long.

If you're part of a reading group, I've added some questions at the back to help start the conversation.

Thank you to everyone that encouraged me along the way.

                    Simon

Prologue

Alexander Lowe was one of the world's most celebrated biochemists, also specialising in many other different scientific fields. His wit and charm earned him an unintentional worldwide following in the 90s, which led to *TIME Magazine* nicknaming him "The Rockstar of Science". Now at fifty eight and well over thirty years into this lifestyle, he was happily repeating the same day over and over with some minor variances.

Professionally, his colleagues held him in high regard. Privately however, whenever anything disturbed his normal happy life, he would feel sudden and extreme aggression, a haunting shadow that lingered from his former life. Thankfully, his loving wife Mary had a talent for helping to suppress these outbursts, like a simmering pan being moved from the hob. There's no question that Mary tamed Alexander after they met, who further matured with age.

Being a rich celebrity brought with it many perks, but those were nothing compared to the contacts he met in the early parts of his life through a secret society he once worked for. After retiring from that part of his life, he retained the perks of the society by becoming one of their clients, identical to many other high profile celebrities. These benefits proved invaluable in creating a perfect artificial life for them. Alexander made sure Mary was not aware of his dealings with the society, including those which were far more sinister and buried in his past.

While cruising through his bespoke life, with every day being comfortingly and numbingly similar to the previous, August 24, 2014, was the day which changed **everything**.

I

Alexander awoke. The sun was gleaming off every reflective surface of the room, filling it with light. He rubbed his eyes softly and clumsily picked up his glasses from the side table. He looked over at the clock, noticing it was very early in the morning and not the routinely 09:30am. Still dazed, he moved his hand towards the other side of the large bed and found only a warm indent on the mattress. Alexander's senses slowly started coming back online as he began hearing retches coming from the ensuite bathroom. He quickly pulled the duvet off and leapt out of the bed to investigate, but before he could reach the door to the bathroom, he felt a warm puddle under his feet which was soaked into the carpet. As he looked down, his sinuses were assaulted with the unmistakable scent of blood. Alexander's eyes widened as adrenaline began pumping through his veins. He threw the door open and saw his wife Mary clinging onto the shower bath, as if she were holding onto it for dear life. Her bloody handprints were scattered all over it and the shower curtain had been torn down onto the floor.

"MARY! WHAT HAPPENED?" screamed Alexander in a panic at the gory sight.

Mary did not answer, she was too focused on the terror that was unfolding within her own body to even acknowledge Alexander's presence. She pulled herself up from her slouching position and threw up into the bathtub, continuing to heave. Alexander began shaking with fear and quickly moved towards her. As he got closer to the bathtub, he saw the deepest shade of red he had ever seen before. He quickly dashed to his mobile phone and called for an ambulance.

The paramedics arrived and attended to Mary before quickly taking her to the local hospital. Alexander followed erratically in his car, narrowly avoiding a collision with another vehicle along the way. As they arrived at the Accident and Emergency department, Alexander parked close by and ran over to the ambulance. They quickly rushed her through the entrance, bypassing others that were waiting to be seen. Alexander eventually caught up with them.

"How is she doing?!" he said, desperately trying to catch his breath.

"Please go to the waiting room, it's through those doors over there." instructed one of the paramedics.

"**No**, I want to be with her!"

A passing male nurse gently patted Alexander's

shoulder with a reassuring smile "Sir please, you'd only get in the way. Let the paramedics do their job, it's for the best."

The conflict within him was overwhelming, but he knew his interference would most likely delay her treatment, even if only by microseconds, so he watched as Mary was carted off down the corridor. The nurse began talking to Alexander, but he could barely hear him, he was fully focused on his own thoughts.

"Sir, please come with me." said the nurse, nudging him in the direction of the waiting room.

He followed the nurse reluctantly, who led him to the waiting room. The terror within him was building, they had been married for nearly thirty years and nothing remotely close to this had happened before, in fact, Mary had always been the perfect picture of health.

"I've spoken to the receptionists, they'll call you over personally when she's ready to be seen." said the busy nurse who quickly left and walked back in the direction they came from.

Alexander began to pace around the waiting room helplessly, not knowing what to do with himself. He began to feel lightheaded, and so took a seat on the chair closest to the door separating himself from the area where the patients were being kept, and where Mary was likely being evaluated. He looked around the sterile room for a distraction, but there wasn't anything captivating other than a few mundane health reminders. He began staring at the door in front of him, studying some of the handwritten notices which were stuck on with tape. He noticed inconsistently sized screws holding the push plates of the door in place. He even began carefully analysing the wooden texture of the door itself. The more Alexander focused on these pointless things, the faster time sped up, which his brain seemed to acknowledge and take full advantage of as a coping mechanism.

An hour passed, and to Alexander it only felt like ten minutes at most. His fixation on the wooden door was now blinding, as if the woodgrain was transforming into different shapes almost psychedelically in his vision. The same male nurse from earlier passed by and noticed the bulging dry red eyes of Alexander, it was a sight he had unfortunately witnessed many times before.

"Sir, would you like me to get you a drink while you wait?"

Alexander whiplashed out of his trippy gaze and quickly turned to the nurse.

"Do you have any news? Mary Lowe. I'm her husband." said Alexander, who did not recognise him as the same nurse as before.

"I'm not looking after her I'm afraid, but she'll be in safe hands though. We have some of the best doctors in the country. I'm sure they'll provide an update soon."

Alexander's worry turned to frustration at the hopelessness of the situation, one outside of his direct control. He looked away from the nurse, clenching his chair with a frighteningly strong adrenaline filled grip, trying his best to put his focus back on what seemed to be the magical door of time. The nurse misread the change in tone and took a seat next to him in an attempt to distract him, putting his clipboard on the small table separating them.

"I wasn't going to say anything, but you're Dr. Lowe, right? There's actually some old science magazines around here with your-"

Before the nurse could even finish his sentence, Alexander, with a frustrated look on his face, took a marker pen out of his jacket pocket and signed his signature on the clipboard. The nurse gave him a defeated look as the pen returned to Alexander's jacket. He stood up, finally understanding Alexander's wish to be left alone and returned to the reception area. He returned moments later and placed a cup of water next to Alexander, which he did not acknowledge. They were once again in two entirely different streams of time.

A couple more hours passed by and the dark thoughts that Alexander had kept restrained were beginning to drip into his mind like a leaking tap. The gaze he had on the door was once again blinding. His composure, his very psyché was slowly cracking and Mary wasn't there to calm him down as she always had been in these high stress situations. His blood pressure was starting to elevate and his heart began pounding dangerously fast and strong. Sweat was beginning to pour down his forehead into his dry eyes. Suddenly the doors flung themselves open, which startled him to his feet, knocking the small cup of water over onto the floor.

"**Mary Lowe!** I'm her husband. Is she okay?" asked Alexander erratically with a dry mouth, unable to control the volume of his voice to the shock of the other people in the waiting room.

"Please come with me," said the doctor in a neutral tone, holding the doors open for him.

Alexander passed through the door, and in an autonomous movement, he quickly felt the texture of the wood, satisfying an urge he didn't know he had. He was led to the room where Mary was being looked after. As he walked in, preparing for the worst, he saw that Mary was sitting up, fully alert and smiling right at him. Alexander breathed a sigh of relief from the deepest pit of his lungs. He rushed beside her and grabbed her hand gently with a returned smile on his face.

"My lovely… how are you feeling?" he asked while gently rubbing her hand.

Mary put her other hand on Alexander's arm and began to rub it, soothing his soul.

"I feel *so* much better, Allie." she said, with a slightly more croakier voice than usual.

"What on Earth happened?" asked Alexander.

Mary's smile turned to a frown for a moment, before it corrected itself.

"They don't know what happened, I still feel a bit nauseous. More importantly, are *you* doing okay?"

Alexander nodded with tears forming in the corner of his eyes "I'm better knowing you're better."

Mary smiled at Alexander, further rubbing his arm.

"The doctors let me have a bit of rest before allowing visitors. I hope you haven't been waiting too long?"

"No, not too long." he said, smiling at her and kissing the back of her hand.

"That's good. Everyone has been so nice to me since I woke up."

Alexander's loving gaze shifted to an analytical stare

at the doctor, who he noticed had been listening to the entire conversation in the corner of the room, waiting for the right moment to interrupt.

"What are the next steps, Doctor?"

The doctor paused for a moment before answering, he was experienced enough to know this was likely not good news based on all the information he had gathered so far.

"We still need to run some further tests. The good news is, as you can see, Mary is alert, awake and feeling better which is very reassuring. However, we're referring her to our oncology department. This wi-" continued the doctor.

As the doctor was talking, the relief in Alexander's face turned back to the vacant stare he had hours previous, he knew what the implications of going to see an oncologist were, they must suspect that Mary has cancer. He twitched his eye in disbelief, his brain was trying its best to not process this piece of information from thoughts into feelings in a feeble attempt to undo what he had just heard. He turned to Mary in disbelief as the doctor was talking, hoping he misheard, but she already had tears running down her face. His spine tingled, his eyes widened in fear as the reality of what was happening crept in. Mary managed to crack a broken smile in a losing effort to reassure Alexander, but her dilated pupils revealed the pure terror trembling beneath the surface, she also knew what this might mean.

"It'll be okay, Allie. I'm... sure they'll have this sorted out soon so don't you worry... okay?" said Mary unconvincingly.

He nodded, noticing his grip on Mary's hand was far too tight. He looked at the doctor who did not share the same optimistic face that Mary had manufactured, which only further heightened his fears.

"Ms. Lowe, is it?" asked a friendly voice from behind them.

They both looked to the direction of the voice, finding an elderly woman waiting in another doorway with a wheelchair.

"I've been asked to take you to oncology dear, it's on the other side of the building so it might take us a little bit to get there. Make sure you wrap up nice and warm, those corridors are bloody cold today."

"Okay, thank you." said Mary, clearing her throat, and wiping her tears with the palm of her hand.

Alexander turned to Mary in a sudden panic.

"This is all happening too fast. It can't be real can it? Please," his voice cracked "Tell me I'm dreaming. I **need** you to tell me none of this is really happening and I'll believe you."

"We'll get through whatever this is, okay?" said Mary in a more serious tone, quickly rubbing his arm.

The porter arrived at Mary's bedside and helped her onto the wheelchair. The doctor handed the porter a thick blue blanket from one of the cabinets, which she covered Mary with.

"Alright, here we go dear!" said the porter in an upbeat tone as she began moving Mary towards the door.

Alexander began to walk behind them out of the room, but the porter looked back at him in disapproval.

"Sorry deary, there's no visitors allowed in oncology, you'll have to go back to the waiting area,"

"But-" said Alexander helplessly before being cut off by the doctor.

"Sorry, you'll need to take a seat in the waiting area again." said the stern-faced doctor, guiding him in the direction that Alexander had originally come from.

The porter slowly pushed Mary through the door, turning left while humming a melody under her breath. Mary looked over her shoulder, waving at Alexander playfully in an attempt to reassure him once again.

"Someone will come and get you when she's ready to be seen again," said the doctor.

Alexander helplessly made his way back to the now

slightly busier waiting room. He noticed his previous seat, the one facing the door was now taken, as were most of the ones surrounding it. To his frustration, he sat much further away from the door, facing away from it. As time passed by, his brain became increasingly starving for a distraction, something to take his mind off his thoughts, but the sick people bickering to each other under their breaths was completely overwhelming. He closed his eyes, put his head in his hands, pulled his grey hair tightly and squeezed his skull to the point where his knuckles turned white under the pressure. The dark thoughts from earlier immediately resumed and started manifesting themselves once again, quickly turning from a leaking tap into a bursting water pipe.

"Oncology… What the fuck are we going to do?" he whispered to himself, before closing his eyes even tighter, feeling the room around him collapsing inward like a black hole, every brick hitting him with full force.

He began reliving the memories of the bloody bathroom, the awful stench of the vomit began shooting through his neurons once again. A small child behind Alexander began to talk very loudly, as he asked his mother for his favourite toy. The mother obliged and pulled a red car from her handbag, which to the child's delight was the exact one he wanted, so he stood up on his seat in excitement. He snatched it from his mother's hand and accidentally hit Alexander in the back of his head with the toy, making Alexander aggressively jolt out of his chair to his feet. Everyone stopped talking and watched as the man stormed towards the toilets frantically like a passing cloud of chaos. He quickly opened the door, nearly ripping it off its hinges and slammed it shut. He grabbed onto the sink for dear life, reminding him immediately of Mary and how she was holding onto the bathtub earlier. He could not escape his thoughts no matter how hard he tried. His brain was torturing him by connecting everything with that horrible sight.

"Get it together, Alexander, calm yourself." he said under his breath, staring at the sink plug.

Without warning, Alexander threw up into the sink, filling it with a mix of mucus, stomach acid and bile. Feeling temporarily better, he looked up at his reflection and was startled to see his father in the mirror, or so he thought. He adjusted his glasses and looked carefully into the mirror as an uncanny valley feeling washed over him. While unpleasant memories of his father began playing out in his mind, he involuntarily rubbed an old faded scar on his cheek. His attention was now entirely fixated on his appearance. Who was this parody looking back at him? He was old, pale, covered in stress lines, his cheeks were bright red, his grey hair was all over the place and his now bloodshot eyes were bulging. Suddenly, a realisation hit him.

"Of course…" he said to himself under his breath. He quickly pulled his phone out of his pocket, which still had the scent of blood on it from earlier. He went to dial Lenny, but instead scrolled up to Hubert instead.

…

Ring ring.

…

"Alexander?"

"Hubert, it's Mary, she's very sick… They're talking about her potentially having cancer." said Alexander erratically.

Hubert was a very prominent figure in the secret society that Alexander once belonged to before becoming a client. The focus of the society, which Alexander had been involved with for decades in one way or another, even before he met Mary, was to help their clients with anything and everything. Whatever Alexander needed, they provided without questioning the intention or motive, no matter how unusual or specific. It was unusual for him to call Hubert, due to his high ranking profile, however, the subject at hand clearly had urgency. He further explained the situation Mary was in and what happened.

"Can you make some calls and get the best doctors on standby?" asked Alexander anxiously.

There was no reply for a moment as Hubert began tapping on his phone.

"I see you're calling from St. Lewis in central London. Is that correct, Alexander?" asked Hubert.

"Yes, that's right."

"Tell them you want to transfer her to Anchorbridge. Lenny will handle the logistics and take it from there." said Hubert before hanging up the call abruptly.

After the call ended, Alexander sat on the toilet for a short time while trying to process his thoughts and plan out the next steps. As he came out of the toilets now much calmer, everyone in the waiting room was now watching him, clearly knowing who he was after gossiping among themselves. Before he could reach the reception counter to request a transfer for Mary, another nurse rushed over.

"Mr. Lowe? We've been looking for you!" said the nurse in a frantic tone.

"What's wrong?!" asked Alexander, matching the demeanour of the nurse.

"It's your wife, please come with me quickly!"

Alexander rushed to the oncology department alongside the nurse, or so he thought. They quickly passed by several hospital staff cleaning the floor which was stained with blood, and suddenly made a quick left to intensive care. Alexander's anxiety and panic began to rise.

"What's going on?!" asked Alexander with a mixture of confusion and anger behind his voice but the nurse did not reply at first "Answer me!" pushed Alexander further.

"She's been taken to intensive care, something happened on the way to the oncology, that's all I've been told."

Alexander picked up the pace and overtook the nurse, going straight through the double doors to the patients area of the ICU. Several nurses, including the receptionist, shouted over at him as he rushed through. He began frantically opening each room until he eventually reached Mary's. What laid before him was a gory sight, a scene straight out of a horror movie. Blood was all over her, including the wheelchair which was next to the bed. The blue blanket that was covering her was now hanging over the wheelchair arm, stained with blood.

"**M-mary?**" asked Alexander as he carefully approached her, but she was totally unconscious. A nurse quickly grabbed his arm to pull him back, but the nurse that led him there piped up.

"It's okay, he's her husband. Can you please stand with me and let them do their job? She's in a serious condition."

"**No!**" shouted Alexander, "I need to transfer Mary to another hospital, to Anchorbridge." he stressed, on the verge of a full blown panic attack.

"There's no way she can leave here in this condition, it's far too dangerous!"

"What are you talking about?!"

The nurse paused, but Alexander's stare demanded further clarification.

"If she keeps bleeding out like this, she won't make it to another hospital."

Alexander felt a sudden coldness overcome him. He tried to speak but words would not come out.

"Please, Sir." said the nurse with a gentle but stern demeanour as other hospital staff began to enter the room.

A week went by, and to the relief of Alexander, Mary was once again stable and communicative, but she was heavily dosed up on a cocktail of drugs to ease the pain and discomfort she had in her stomach. The secret society had secured Mary her own private room using its influence. They also convinced hospital management to allow him to stay by her side even throughout the night which was usually strictly against the rules. During one of the nights, Mary was woken by Alexander.

"Allie, what are you doing?" asked Mary groggily.

Alexander was standing next to a cupboard in the private room, staring at it as if he was contemplating opening it. This wasn't an unusual sight to her, as Alexander had been having an increasing amount of night terrors and episodes of sleep walking over the last couple of months, which she assumed was due to the stress he was experiencing at work. What did startle her however was the lighting in the room, which presented Alexander as a dark silhouette.

"*I* am just working on… something… Do not worry, *I* am quite awake…" said Alexander with a slight growl to his voice.

"You always say that you goofball, come back here. It's probably really late."

Alexander sighed and slowly shuffled across the room back to the chair he had been sleeping in next to her. As he made his way back, he never once looked at her. As he closed his eyes, she attempted to place her hand on his shoulder lovingly, but he instinctively jolted back, before falling asleep again almost instantly.

The next day, Alexander had no memory of sleepwalking, and Mary knew better than to tell him about it as she knew it made him feel very self-conscious. His fear for Mary's health was growing stronger. He had never seen her this weak before, but he knew he had to remain optimistic.

...

Knock knock.

The young doctor that had been looking after Mary for the last week came through the door.

"Hi Mary, Alexander. How are we both doing?"

"Do you have any news yet?" asked Alexander abruptly, standing to his feet.

"Allie, please. Sorry doctor, yes we're doing well thanks. We were just watching a bit of telly, Cosmos, it's one of our favourite shows."

The doctor did not match the playful energy of Mary and changed the subject to the matter at hand.

"I do have some news to share… I'm afraid."

The tension in the room immediately thickened as the doctor took a seat next to them. Alexander turned the TV off and sat down next to Mary once again, holding her hand tightly.

"Go on." said Mary, waiting for the news that was

seemingly about to change their lives forever.

"I'll get straight to the point. You have adenocarcinomas, it's a form of stomach cancer."

...

Mary looked at Alexander in shock, but he was completely focused on the doctor. He had already envisioned this moment hundreds of times in his head over the last week, preparing for the worst.

"What are the treatment options?" asked Alexander, trying to quickly take control of the situation.

The young doctor sighed under his breath, playing with the wedding ring on his finger.

"Look... I'm not going to paint a nice picture here." said the doctor, turning to Mary "We've looked at the results very carefully. The cancer is extremely aggressive, it's at stage four, it's terminal. It's already spread from your stomach to your liver. There's nothing we can do to stop it from spreading further at its current rate."

Alexander stood up in anger, throwing the chair backwards from under him.

"I've been telling you to transfer Mary to Anchorbridge for the last week, they'd be able to treat her!"

"Alexander, I've already spoken with your doctors

numerous times. I actually just got off the phone with them before coming here, we all looked at the same results and all of us agreed it was best to keep her here. The diagnosis is conclusive." said the doctor, once again turning to Mary "We'd expect two months in the best case scenario. I'm **really** sorry."

The bluntness of the doctor, along with the suddenness of this information began to boil Alexander's brain, making it process far beyond his limits.

"For fucks sake..." said Alexander, slowly pacing towards the doctor.

"Allie... Hey..." said Mary sternly, turning to him.

"Are you really telling me you can't do **ANYTHING?!**" screamed Alexander who was now in the doctor's face.

"I wish I had better news, I really do. The cancer is far too aggressive for even our most experimental treatments. We've never seen it spread so fast."

"You need to talk to **MY** doctors again! There's no way they agreed to keep Mary in this shithole!" shouted Alexander even louder, grabbing his phone out of his pocket, pacing back towards Mary's side.

"Allie please..."

"We've wasted a week in this fucking cesspit of a hospital and **THIS** is the news you give us? We're doing nothing but wasting precious time here." said Alexander, pressing the incorrect buttons on his phone in a frenzy.

"**ALEXANDER!**" shouted a weakened Mary, grabbing his arm with what little strength she had.

He turned to Mary, lowering his phone and snapped out of his blind rage.

"It's... **okay**..."

The spine tingling feeling he had experienced before returned and shot right up to Alexander's brain. He looked at her, his emotions swinging like a pendulum back and forth between erupting anger and a pit of sadness before the realisation finally hit him. His face erupted with a lake of tears as he began to cry hysterically. Mary pulled him in close, also crying deeply into his shoulder.

"I'll give you both some time... Once again, I'm so, so sorry. I wish we could do something."

The doctor, who was on the verge of tears himself, closed the curtains around the bed and quickly left the private room.

As the days passed, Alexander stuck by Mary's side, often laying beside her in the bed cuddling and talking about their treasured memories. Privately, he had been in constant discussions with Lenny from the secret society about the potential of replacing their doctors at the hospital with his own. Mary and Alexander spent time playing their favourite board games, watching their favourite TV shows and spending a considerable amount of time scheming how to sneak in some of Mary's favourite cheeky foods.

"I could go and get us a pizza from Andolini's if you'd like?" asked Alexander, checking his phone to see if they were open.

"Oh Andolini's… it's been such a long time since we've had that, that would be lovely."

"Is your stomach up to it?" asked Alexander, looking up from his phone, after briefly reading some logistical texts from Lenny.

Mary nodded, although she was not hungry in the slightest, she knew it would make them both happy to have one of their favourite meals ever once again even if it was just the sight of the box.

"I'm sure I'll have a slice by the time it arrives, they always take so long to deliver." chuckled Mary.

"Remember the last time we had it? It took them three hours to deliver it because they couldn't find our new house." joked Alexander.

Mary smiled and nodded again, gesturing a laugh but unable to do so.

"Do they even deliver this far away?"

"It looks like they do, I could probably meet them in

the car park."

Mary's eyes lit up at the news, which made Alexander smile.

"Now that's something I haven't seen in a little while." she said with a returned smile.

Alexander placed his hand on hers and looked lovingly into her eyes, which she returned.

"Allie, I don't say this enough" she said, looking down with guilt "But I'm so... so-"

Mary immediately jolted up, with a terrified look on her face.

"Mary?" asked a startled Alexander.

She grabbed onto Alexander's shirt with great force and threw up thick dark red blood and bile all over him. She looked at him with a terror he had never seen from her before as the life drained from her eyes. She suddenly lost consciousness and let go of him, falling back onto her pillow. He slammed the emergency button and a loud siren began to echo throughout the room and down the corridor.

"SOMEONE HELP! QUICK! SOMEONE!!!"

Mary began seizing violently, throwing up once again but this time all over herself in the same dark red bile and blood mixture. The nurses and doctor ran in and quickly checked her vitals.

"She has no pulse!" shouted a nurse to the doctor.

"Defibrillator **NOW!**" replied the doctor, gesturing at it behind one of the nurses.

The nurse rushed over with the defibrillator, put it on Mary's chest and began trying to resuscitate her.

"CLEAR!"

Alexander looked on in horror, tightly holding his head with both of his hands. His mouth was wide open at the horror unfolding before his eyes.

"CLEAR!"

Nothing happened.

"One more time!"

"Clear!"

Nothing again.

...

The young doctor looked up at the clock.

"20:52"

He turned to Alexander with sadness in his eyes.

"N-n.. no. We were jus- we… were…"

Alexander's face began twitching as if a thousand different painful emotions hit him all at once like shrapnel. He looked down at the blood which was soaked into his clothes and covered his hands. The smell suddenly hit him, but amplified tenfold and it was far worse than the previous occurrence. His entire body began rumbling to its core in pure uncontrollable adrenaline like he had never experienced before which was only multiplying with every second that passed. He grabbed onto the curtain that was surrounding the hospital bed and began panting incredibly fast.

"Sir!" shouted one of the nurses with concern.

Alexander groaned in agony as he clutched his chest. He began knocking over everything around him in a moment of crazed madness. Suddenly, as if an off-switch was pressed, he fell over and smashed his face into the floor with immense force, breaking his glasses in the process.

II

Alexander awoke. The sun was gleaming off every reflective surface of the room, filling it with light. Dazed, he looked at the clock, but it wasn't where he expected it to be. His eyes began searching for it, instead finding it in the corner of the room. He could only vaguely make it out, it was 09:30am. He sighed in relief.

"Thank goodness." he thought, feeling as if his entire brain had reset itself to its factory settings. He closed his eyes again and moved his hand to the left, only to find an unfamiliar cold railing on the edge of a hospital bed. The realisation hit him like a truck. He quickly sat up using the little adrenaline that was available to him.

"Mary? **MARY?**" screamed Alexander as his memories began flooding back to him. The pain, both physical and emotional, was suddenly overwhelming as the initial high of the adrenaline wore off.

The room began to darken as his dreamy illusions cleared. He quickly realised he was not at home, he was in fact in a dimly lit hospital ward and the clock actually showed 4am. The other patients on the ward were now wide awake after Alexander's outburst. The female nurse who was looking after him rushed over.

"Mr. Lowe? You're awake?!" whispered the nurse in surprise.

"Mary? Is she okay?" asked Alexander loudly. His face was pleading for answers that contradicted his returning memories, which he hoped were just a nightmare.

"Mr. Lowe… I'm sorry. I'm afraid your wife passed away last night."

Alexander looked at the nurse in horror. His lower lip began twitching uncontrollably as he tried to communicate that she must be mistaken. He could, under no circumstance, accept the reality of the situation, this **had** to be a nightmare.

"You're incredibly lucky to be alive. The stress you went through increased your blood pressure rapidly, causing a blood clot that resulted in a stroke. It's a miracle you're even awake so soon after an event like that so please… try to rest, okay?"

Alexander attempted to get out of the hospital bed but it was no use, his body was a shell of its former self, as if an explosion had torn and ripped him to shreds internally.

"I **will not** accept this. You **are** mistaken." he said under his breath as he became hyper focused on his own thoughts.

The nurse looked at Alexander sombrely.

"Is there anything I can do for you?" asked the nurse

as she sat on the end of the bed with sympathy.

Alexander's brain was roaring internally, trying to process a million puzzle pieces together simultaneously.

...

He cleared his throat.

"Mary, she... told me she didn't want to donate her organs."

...

The nurse paused for a moment before responding. This wasn't a normal thing to bring up under the circumstances.

"Excuse me?"

"She changed her mind, just before she got sick."

"Alexander, please. We can discuss this later in the morning. It's just after 4am... we have to be respectful of the other patients." said the nurse, motioning to the other beds around them.

"Please..." pleaded Alexander helplessly.

The nurse looked at him with empathy before sighing briefly.

"Look, this is something the doctor asked me to talk

to you about if by some miracle you were awake and alert today. Her donor card has instructed us to donate any healthy organs, so they're going to be removing them later today."

"No. You can't... She wrote it down at home but we never got a chance to update the registry."

"This isn't something that the family can normally veto at this point, it's-"

"Please... you can't take them. It'd be against her wishes."

The nurse once again sighed, knowing that she had very limited options if what Alexander was saying was correct.

"Alright Alexander, but you will need to provide the paperwork indicating her consent withdrawal, and it'll have to be very quickly."

"I'll have it for you later today."

"Okay Alexander, we can help you call someone. Just try to get some sleep and focus on your recovery. I know it probably feels impossible, but your body desperately needs it."

"Where is she now?" asked Alexander, ignoring the instructions of the nurse.

She looked at him defeated, knowing full well that he wasn't going to listen.

"She's currently in the hospital morgue."

Alexander sat himself up slowly, which was an enormous effort. He moved his hands backwards to a notepad and pen that were placed on the bedside table.

"I want you to release her to Ronson's Funeral Directors immediately, please do not delay." instructed Alexander.

He picked up the notepad and pen with an incredible struggle, trying to get used to his newly weakened hands. After a few minutes and several failed attempts, he handed her a jittery note with a phone number on it.

"This is their number, can you call them now urgently? They will answer."

…

The nurse once again paused with a look of confusion as she took the note from his shaky hand. Internally she was trying to figure out how he had a funeral director's telephone number memorised.

"Alright… I wouldn't normally do this but it's not like you can do much in your current condition and we need to act quickly if Mary had changed her mind before she passed."

"Promise me you'll call them right now, they work

24/7." insisted Alexander.

The nurse had even more questions, but she knew she had to wrap this up for the sake of the other patients and their sleep.

"I promise. We'll call them now, okay? You'll need to get your family to bring in the paperwork later today though." said the nurse, patting Alexander's leg gently with a reassuring smile.

The nurse stood up and began to close the curtain around Alexander's bed.

"Please, try to get some rest. We need to do a lot more tests on you later in the morning." said the nurse as she left to pass on the information to the doctor and the morgue.

Later that morning, the same nurse returned before the end of her shift. She pulled the curtain to the side, revealing an empty bed. Alexander wasn't there. She checked around the ward, but found no sign of him and nobody had seen him leave either. Shortly after their discussion in the middle of the night, Alexander had slowly snuck out of the hospital and miraculously drove himself to a nearby motel where he checked in and made a call.

Knock knock… knock.

II

Alexander limped his way to the motel door in his hospital gown. He removed the lock from the latch and took a seat back down on the edge of the bed. The stroke had significantly reduced the ability of his muscles in his left leg in particular. A tall well built bald man in a maroon suit opened the door, he was holding a tan briefcase and a cane.

"Lenny." said Alexander, nodding in approval.

Lenny, still standing in the doorway, threw the cane towards Alexander, but his reflexes didn't cooperate and the cane fell in front of him.

"Christ, you look like absolute shit." said Lenny, closing the door behind himself. He walked in and picked the cane up off the floor and passed it to Alexander carefully.

Alexander took the cane reluctantly and was visibly frustrated that he would have to rely on it

Lenny and Alexander were childhood friends, and Alexander was responsible for bringing him into the secret society that Lenny was still an active member of. He laid the tan briefcase on a side table and unlocked it, taking out a purple battered A4 journal which had an embossed reflective Silver crest featuring a vulture on the front. He then passed Alexander a new set of glasses, an exact duplicate of the ones he had broken when he fell.

"I didn't take you for a motel sort of guy." joked Lenny, looking around the dark dingy room.

"The alternative wasn't preferable." said Alexander, putting on his new glasses.

Lenny looked down at Alexander who was hunched forwards on the edge of the bed.

"I'm sorry to hear about Mary, Champ... My guys have already cleaned both the bedroom and bathroom for you."

"Thank you, Lenny."

"Hubert briefed me on what happened along with the requirements you passed onto him." said Lenny while taking a seat next to the bed, opening the journal and placing it on his lap while crossing his legs.

"I've had my guys work on the document to forge Mary's donor consent. It surprisingly required an apostille stamp which made things a little more complicated. You'd think a stamp would be easy to fake or bypass, but it bears a specific reference number which is going to be checked by the hospital."

"Certainly," replied Alexander in agreement.

"So, we used an existing reference number from the government apostille database earlier today while simulating a full scale attack on all of their services to distract IT department's focus. To summarise, the apostille number is legitimate, one already used however."

"Won't using an existing number be suspicious?"

"Normally, yes. Luckily their IT department has plenty of unused real reference numbers that they configured while building the apostle stamp database many years ago, so it won't look out of the ordinary using one of those. They don't have the best of practices so they won't notice, and when they do, years down the line, they'll think it was an administrative mistake."

"Impressive." said Alexander, standing himself up with his new cane.

Lenny watched on as Alexander began to slowly pace around the room.

"Your other requirement is a lot more complex but we're working on it. The hospital contacted the number you gave them. In short, we should receive Mary's body later today. We're going to preserve it using the method you passed on to Hubert. Remember, that number was a one-time use." said Lenny, pulling a stack of silvery business cards out of his suit pocket. "Under the circumstances, I understand why you couldn't give us a heads up with who might be calling. But in future, do so, alright?" said Lenny sternly, passing one of the cards to Alexander, who nodded and took it.

"Memorise that new number. You know-"

"Yes, yes, I remember the process for goodness sake," interrupted Alexander, taking the card "I'll memorise it."

Lenny put the remaining business cards away in his pocket.

"So, Hubert said you had another requirement, one that you wanted to discuss in person?" asked Lenny, grabbing a silver pen from inside his journal.

Alexander let out a deep sigh, still pacing around the room trying to get used to the cane.

"Yes, it's about my lab. I'm going to need a lot of… new equipment and literature. It's going to look very strange to the finance department, but I need it to look legitimate."

"Shouldn't be too much trouble, we've done this plenty of times for our other clients as I'm sure you remember." said Lenny with a smile "We can modify the invoices and set up a fake supplier. It helps that you work for the government these days, they are so careless that they won't even notice and even if they did, we have new systems in place to mitigate that." said Lenny pausing briefly "Those invoices though… they'll need to come through us…" he said, pausing again mid thought, making very quick shorthand notes in the leather journal that only he could read "Yeah, actually, this will be very straight forward. I'll liaise with one of my guys and get back to you with the finer details."

"Thank you again, Lenny."

"Alright then…" said Lenny, closing his journal and placing it back into his tan briefcase. "You know how to reach me if you need anything else."

Alexander nodded once again.

Lenny picked up his things and looked over at Alexander with concern.

"Take care of yourself, alright Champ?"

"You too, Lenny."

Lenny opened the door and left as abruptly as he entered.

The next day, Alexander was back at work, slowly making his way down the corridor to the common room in a catatonic state. A colleague passed by and noticed him with his new cane.

"Alex? What happened? Are you okay?" asked a voice piercing the static noise in Alexander's mind.

"Yes Rita, I'm doing well thank you. I've just injured my leg, it's nothing serious." said Alexander, still limping in the same direction away from her.

Alexander hadn't slept since he woke up in the

hospital and it was starting to take its toll on both his body and mind. His keen focus, the mask keeping him together throughout the trauma, was starting to slip every second he was awake and it wouldn't take much for the people around him to notice, especially as he was renowned for his usual cheery upbeat nature. The radio underneath his lab coat suddenly went off, to his relief.

"Delivery at the rear entrance for Dr. Lowe, signature and collection required." said a dampened static voice.

Alexander turned around and began to make his way in a different direction, passing by Rita who for a brief moment thought she saw an imposter, someone parodying Alexander.

"Do you need a hand with the delivery?"

"No." said Alexander abruptly, slowly continuing onward away from her in the opposite direction.

"Was that really Alex?" she thought. The cold focus in his eyes made her feel very uneasy, as if the air around him was pulsating with negative energy.

Alexander, now with a portable dolly in tow, arrived at the back entrance of the building twenty minutes later. Waiting at the rear of the lorry were two delivery men, henchmen of Lenny. They each had the same silver vulture on their clothing as Lenny had on his journal and pen, but as a metal pin instead. Alexander's eyes suddenly widened when he saw a crate emerge from the lorry, he knew what this was.

"Mary…" said Alexander under his breath. His pupils dilated as he tried to catch the breath that had just escaped his lungs "Be **very** careful with that crate." he instructed firmly while clenching his fist.

"Understood, Dr. Lowe. There's a couple more in here for you as well." said one of the delivery drivers as they began lowering the large crate onto the portable dolly. He escorted both them and the crate to his office and unlocked the door. When the men entered the room they were taken back by how sterile, tidy and bare it was, like a furniture showroom. The only things that occupied the room were a computer, a desk, two chairs and a bookcase.

"Come inside, and make sure the door closes behind you."

As they carefully pushed the crate into the office, distracted with the room furnishings, or lack thereof, the crate lightly grazed against the edge of the doorframe. Alexander saw this and quickly moved in front of the delivery man.

"Listen to me very carefully because I am ***not*** going to tell either of you again. Be careful with that crate. Do you understand?" he said in a menacingly darker tone.

"Our apologies, Dr. Lowe." replied the delivery man as the door behind them closed on its own, locking automatically.

Alexander continued to stare at them for a few moments, before eventually breaking his cold gaze. He made his way to the bookcase and unclipped something metallic behind it. He then stepped back briefly and moved it to the side with ease using the previously unseen rails that were holding it in place. As the bookcase moved to the side, it revealed a thick metal door. The delivery men looked at each other comically and grinned, realising they just witnessed a secret room revealed behind a bookcase. Alexander unlocked the metal door with his keys and pushed it open with his shoulder. As the door opened all the way, an abyss of darkness greeted them, and a chilling breeze blew throughout the small office. Alexander pulled a string which flooded the darkness with light, revealing an aged custom made elevator with rusted exposed gears and a thick metal grate for a floor. Alexander stepped onto the creaky grate of the elevator and signalled them over eagerly. The men's previously grinning faces instantaneously turned to horror at the deathtrap of the precarious elevator that laid before them, knowing they had no option but to stand on it with him. They mustered up the courage and pushed the crate carefully onto the elevator.

II

As the last two wheels curbed onto the grated floor, the elevator began making roaring noises which echoed all around them and deep down into the shaft below them.

"Will this do?" whispered one of the trembling delivery men to the other.

Alexander poked his finger hard into the chest of the delivery driver who asked the question, right above the silver pin.

"You will do everything I say. I'll release you of your duties when we're done here. Got it?" he instructed, slamming a red button with the back of his hand in a sudden sign of strength.

The tenseness of the situation was only magnified when a cascade of lights began turning on individually down the shaft below them, revealing the cold hungry depths that they felt could easily swallow them whole at any moment. As soon as all the lights were finished turning on, the elevator began descending. The nervous delivery drivers held onto each other for stability. After around thirty seconds, the final light passed by above them and the shaft became pitch black. Suddenly without warning the elevator clanked down hard as it reached the bottom, making the two delivery men stumble over each other. Alexander carefully stepped off the elevator and pulled another string, lighting up another metal door in front of them. He pulled out his keys once again and unlocked it. As the door pushed open, Alexander's large secret laboratory lit up automatically. This was just as sterile and tidy as the office above but significantly colder, to the point where their breath was visible as it left their mouths.

"Put the crate onto that bench over there." instructed Alexander, pointing to the other side of the lab.

The men wheeled the crate across the room and began raising it onto the workbench, gently placing it down as instructed.

"Bring the others here please."

They both looked at each other with concern.

"How do we…?" enquired one of the delivery men, looking at the elevator behind them through the door.

"Just get back on the elevator." barked Alexander, pushing them towards it with his cane "Make sure the door in my office closes behind you so nobody walks in while you're getting the others."

Alexander hit the red button, lighting up the shaft once again, sending them back up to his office. They began swearing to each other under their breaths with worry as it began to creak with each movement. He closed the metal door behind him and sighed to himself with some relief as their contagious anxiety was temporarily removed from the room. The room was now eerily silent, a silence so quiet that he could hear his own heartbeat, which now sounded oddly different to the last time he was in the lab. He ignored it and began to hobble his way towards his computer, turning it on. While he was waiting for the computer to boot up, tears began involuntarily pouring down his face to his surprise.

"Wha..." he whispered to himself, touching his cheek in disbelief.

He looked over to the crate.

...

The realisation hit him, this was the first time since just before her death that he was alone with Mary. He shook his head slowly, letting out a deep growl of sadness and clenched the desk as hard as his weak body would allow him.

"You don't... deserve any of this..." he said, clearing his throat as best as he could "This is just temporary, I swear. I'll make sure we see each other properly again very soon... I... just need a bit of time, okay? Just... rest for now my lovely. I have a plan." he said, clearing his throat a second time and wiped the tears away before returning back to his cold composure.

"Computer"

beep

"Create a new project and record a log."

"Project 807 has been closed. Folder number 808 has been created. Log 1 - Recording"

...

Project #: *808*
Encrypted Log Entry: *1*
Date & Time*: September 5, 2014, 10:41*
Log:

*We need to collect our thoughts... We haven't slept in some time. There's a lot to process, a lot to do. So please listen very carefully, Alexander. There's no doubt in our mind that her body in its current state can be brought back to life. Her neurons are still there, just not firing, her heart is still there, just not pumping. Mary, as we know her, is still there, just dormant, waiting to be awakened again. I-**we** just need to figure out how to undo the death signal that spread itself throughout her body. It **is** possible. We **know** we can do it.*

There is of course the obvious problem of the cancer which would just... kill her body again if we reanimated her. Luckily Silver, specifically Lenny, got to Mary before the body could decompose. They preserved her body as we instructed.

Thank goodness...

We now need to put her into a more permanent cryogenic freeze before she decays using the equipment that Lenny's team is going to be bringing down to the lab shortly.

*The stroke, no doubt, has critically fractured our body internally and we fear our days are now numbered. We don't feel ourselves anymore and not just physically. Something else is different, **something else** has changed, but we can't put our finger on it.*

Alexander looked up at his second computer monitor and noticed the delivery men were waiting at his office door with the remaining crates.

Alexander sighed, "Computer, end recording."
beep

Alexander pressed a button, which unlocked his office door upstairs. The men pushed the remaining crates through, ensuring that the door locked behind them. They made their way down the jittery elevator.

"Okay Dr. Lowe. That should do it." said one of the men, putting the last remaining crate on one of the other benches, clearly shaken by the whole experience but relieved it was over.

"No." snapped Alexander immediately "What did I tell you earlier?"

The men stood there dumbfounded as Alexander handed them a crowbar each.

"Open them."

They once again looked at each other confused but nodded in agreement, proceeding to the first crate they brought in.

"No. I'll open that one myself. Focus on the others and hurry it up."

The men started opening the crates, getting the equipment out and carefully putting it all together. Once completed, they moved it into one of the corners of the lab. They had no clue what any of this strange equipment was for and they found this whole situation very strange. It was clear that the main piece of equipment was some sort of machine that someone could lay in though, but that's all they could piece together.

"You may leave now. Pass on my thanks to Lenny."

instructed Alexander.

The men exited up the elevator and out of the office, leaving the premises as fast as they could before Alexander could give them another uncomfortable task. As Alexander watched the men leave on the monitor, he turned it off and slowly swivelled his chair to the final remaining crate and stared at it for a few moments. With a shaking hand, Alexander grabbed one of the crowbars that was left on the bench. He cranked it open, revealing a small black body bag matching Mary's petite frame. Industrial coolants were padded all around both the box and the lid which allowed the contents to be frozen in place. The lab was cold, but it was nothing like the inside of this box. Alexander knew he was against the clock as soon as the crate opened up so he immediately unzipped the bag revealing Mary's cold lifeless body.

...

Alexander stopped in his tracks. His heartbeat began pounding like a drum in his ear, which was deafening in the silent lab. He covered his mouth slowly with a trembling hand, noticing the shaking spread throughout his entire body uncontrollably like a chain reaction. He grabbed onto the edge of the bench as the weight of what he was doing and everything that had happened recently fell onto his shoulders like a slab of concrete. The mask had finally fallen.

"N-no-I jus-" he tried to get words out but they became mumbled garbage. He felt a pit of vomit building up in his stomach.

"I ju ca-" his second attempt was even worse, his entire body was now quaking violently, not helped by the ice cold box underneath him.

"Please... Help me," he whispered to himself helplessly as he closed his eyes tightly.

In an autonomous action, he placed his left hand gently on his right arm. A familiar calmness began washing over him from unknown origin. He looked at his arm in surprise as he breathed out deeply, which created a thick vapour cloud above the cold crate. The urgency of what he had to do returned as did his focus.

"It won't be long now, my lovely. I'm just... moving you somewhere more comfortable..."

With his newly found composure, he carefully picked up her stiff light body, positioning it into the newly installed cryogenic pod. He inserted multiple wires and tubes into her body. He set the temperature to the default setting of -130°C and took a long glance at Mary before closing the pod door and turning the machine on. He turned to another of the newly installed machines next to the pod and pressed some buttons, which began to generate liquid nitrogen behind a glass door. He stumbled over to the computer once again and sat down in his chair ready to resume the recording. He sat there for a few moments, but found that he was quickly losing consciousness, the sleep deprivation had finally caught up to him, accelerated by the stressful situation. Before he even realised he was losing consciousness, he was quickly snatched out of reality.

III

Alexander awoke in a pitch black void.

He could not breathe.

He began to panic hysterically and pushed against the sandy but firm ground, surfacing from the heavy red sand that had been covering him. He immediately coughed up a large amount of the sand and began gasping for air as if it was his first breath. He tried to stand up but the sand was still firmly clamped around his ankles, so he fell backwards. He looked around in a frenzy, seeing a red desert in all directions. He began rubbing the sand grains from his eyes, which was causing him a significant amount of pain, as if his eyeballs were being grinded with sandpaper.

"W-what the.." he said as he looked up at the haunting orange sky above him which was littered with white cracks that extended far into the distance and across some of the ground further on in the horizon.

The cracks took on the appearance of lightning but they were a permanent fixture. The more he stared at them, the closer they resembled neuron pathways in the brain. A strange humming noise began to increase in volume all around him. As Alexander moved his hand under the sand's surface to stand himself up again, he felt every grain of sand on his fingertips, not only that, he felt something solid under the surface. He began digging with his hands but in the process punctured his fingers with splinters. He pulled his hand back in pain.

"This isn't a dream, it... feels too real." he said while pulling out several large splinters with his fingertips "How did I get here?"

Alexander carefully resumed digging and pulled up a door handle that was attached to a broken piece of wood. He looked around the surrounding area more clearly after removing more of the sand from his eyes. He noticed that there were smashed doors, handles and screws littered across the landscape in every direction. He looked back at the door handle that he had dug up and examined it closely. It was clearly blown off a door recently from the scorch marks surrounding the wood. The pleasant smell of burning wood was thick in the air. Alexander finally managed to get to his feet and unanchored himself from the sand.

"HELLO?" shouted Alexander into the distance, but no reply came.

The cracks in the sky widened briefly, lighting up the landscape with an intense heat, which kicked up a small dust cloud beneath him.

"Is… anyone there?" he asked, while brushing the sand off his lab coat.

He began to pace forward through the desert in a seemingly random direction, walking past multiple large jagged pieces of broken doors. Suddenly flaming pieces of wood began falling around him. He instinctively covered his head, which was wise, as he began to get barraged with waves of screws and other sharp objects, some of which bounced off him. Once the dust settled, he noticed a large door had fallen in front of him, which was still alight at the edges, it had a number written on it in bright red blood.

"808"

"Allie!" cried out a familiar voice from above him which gripped his attention away from the unusual door. He looked up at the sky anxiously.

"**Mary?** ARE YOU THERE?"

He looked around but there was nothing, just an eerie silence as the humming began to fade away. Suddenly, the white cracks in the sky began to creak loudly as they sealed themselves shut, showing no sign they were ever there. He felt his body ache all over, making him clutch at his torso, which to his horror was now soaked in blood and bile. He recognised his appearance, it was how he looked just after

Mary had died in front of him. The pleasant smell of wood was replaced with the thick unpleasant odour from that fateful day. Alexander's heart rate began to skyrocket as the blood began to drip down from his hands onto the sand's surface, making it sizzle slightly on impact. The humming returned and intensified.

"SOMEONE HELP ME, PLEASE!" he screamed out into the desert.

Suddenly silence, total and absolute. The landscape started eclipsing, increasing with darkness until there was only a slight ghostly white glow on the sand's surface.

"... save me..." echoed Mary's voice softly and clearly in his right ear.

He felt a reassuring hand on his right arm.

...

Alexander shot up from his desk in an intense panic, covered in sweat, as if he had awoken from a nightmare. The humming was still present, which startled him, so he quickly turned in the direction it was coming from, noticing it was the machine that Mary was laying in. It was pumping cryoprotectant into her body on a now regular cycle. He checked the clock and it was 07:15am the next day. He sat there for a few moments while catching his breath. He stood up and began walking towards the machine, forgetting his cane in the process. As he made his first step, he instantly fell over onto his hip, causing him to groan in significant pain. He slowly pulled himself up with whatever strength he had, using the desk as a support. In pure frustration he ripped the keyboard from his desk and threw it across the room, smashing it against the wall. He picked his cane up and began frantically hobbling towards the elevator to escape the lab. As he exited, he glanced over at the cryogenic pod with heavy bloodshot eyes and slammed the metal door shut in anger, which echoed loudly up the elevator shaft.

The time during and after the funeral was critical for Alexander as he knew he had to keep up appearances with not just their family and friends, but most importantly under the circumstances, his co-workers. The funeral, for Alexander, held no significance, as he knew she was going to be by his side again very soon. His full focus throughout the ceremony was on the red desert and the door. The entire vision kept replaying in his mind, interrupting all of his thoughts. He had never experienced a nightmare that felt so real. It was as if Mary was crying out to him directly from within the cryogenic pod, as if the door was separating them in some way.

III

After the funeral, the news of Mary's passing began to spread due to Alexander's high profile. He returned to work once again after a couple of days, venturing into the common room, where he saw two of his employees sitting and talking. He proceeded to the kettle and boiled some water, putting two teaspoons of coffee into his usual cup. As the kettle boiled, he stared at the granules in the jar. The mysterious red desert was still very present in mind as if it was somehow calling out for his immediate return. Whenever Alexander's mind wandered there, he'd begin to sweat profusely. He felt like his brain was processing information like a supercomputer at all times, taking an immense toll on his body. His team began whispering to themselves, looking over at him with curiosity and concern. Alexander could feel the atmosphere in the room building, which was interfering with his own thoughts. The kettle clicked, and he poured the boiling water into the cup before manufacturing a neutral expression on his face.

"Hi team." said Alexander while hobbling over to them in an upbeat tone with his cane in one hand and his coffee cup in the other.

"Hey Alex… how are you holding up?" asked Rita, showing concern.

"Ah… Some days are easier than others." said

Alexander, taking a seat next to them. He began stirring the black coffee with his spoon.

"We're here if you want to talk, you know that right?" insisted Peter.

"I appreciate that Pete, I really do. Did anything happen in my absence?"

"Not really, same old... Oh actually, the New York office sent out a memo saying they found something of interest in the specimen they examined."

"Oh?" asked Alexander, moving his hands around the cup as it got hotter in his hands.

"Yeah but you know how overly excited those yanks get over nothing," chuckled Peter. "We're going to check over their results and try to reproduce the result later today."

"Sounds good" said Alexander, sipping some of his piping hot coffee while looking around the room "Where's Francis?"

Rita rolled her eyes as she looked at Peter. She shook her head in frustration.

"Where do you think?" she asked sarcastically.

"Surely not. He called in sick again?" asked Alexander in disappointment.

"Who knows? Whenever you're not around he just makes up any excuse to avoid the office." said Rita in frustration.

"He's such a fucking leech, seriously, can't we get rid of him yet?" exploded Peter.

Alexander watched Peter closely as he let out his frustrations, examining his body language closely before returning back to his upbeat self. This analytical cross examination was second nature to him from his previous tenure at the secret society when he was one of their members. He looked down at his coffee cup.

"It's not as easy as that, Pete. You know how much of a nightmare it is firing anyone these days. He knows how to play the system." said Alexander, taking another sip.

"I know, but it just means we have to cover for him all the time. He's a real piece of shit." said Pete, leaning back in his seat in frustration.

Alexander nodded at his cup while a small humorous smile crept on his face, which Rita immediately noticed.

"It's good to see you smile, Alex." said Rita with a reassuring smile of her own.

Alexander looked at Rita in surprise. He was reminded of Mary's last moments in the hospital where she said something similar.

"I'm going to be okay, thank you both."

A large clank was heard outside the common room as Francis barged in suddenly, carrying his usual battered shopping bag. He ignored everyone in the room and proceeded to the fridge, dropping the bag loudly onto the countertop. He put a can of pop and a microwave meal into the fridge while leaving a trail of mud on the ground from his shoes.

"Nice of you to join us!" shouted Peter across the room, still sitting back in his seat with his arms folded.

"Yeah… big smash on the motorway, was stuck in traffic for over an hour!"

"Where have you been for the last few days, Francis?" enquired Alexander.

Francis stopped what he was doing and looked at Alexander, finally acknowledging him.

"Could ask the same of you, couldn't I?" snapped Francis as he continued to put what seemed like a week's worth of items into the fridge.

The room went quiet, Francis either didn't know or he didn't care, regardless, the tension in the room could be cut with a knife and Alexander was staring right through Francis like a wolf eyeing up his next meal.

"You're late, so make up the time at the end of the day. Understood?"

"Yeah, sure thing mate." replied Francis sarcastically, putting the now empty shopping bag into his back pocket. He quickly exited the room leaving the fridge open, stamping more mud into the carpeted floor.

As Alexander looked back at his team, Rita was showing Peter a traffic report for the area on her phone, which showed no incidents on the motorway.

"He's fucking unbelievable." sighed Peter in disbelief.

"Thank you both for covering for me and Francis," said Alexander, changing the subject back.

"Hey, it's all good Alex, we're a team. But… should you even be back so soon?" asked a still concerned Rita.

"There's no better distraction for me than work, you both know me."

Rita smiled once again, unconvinced, but nodded in agreement.

"Anyway, I need to get to work, there's a lot I need to catch up with. It's nice seeing you both." said Alexander, downing the remainder of his hot coffee. He stood himself up with his cane and walked over to the sink to rinse his cup. As he went to leave the room, he slammed the fridge door shut that Francis had left open.

As he approached his office door, he noticed how eerily similar it was in appearance to the one from his vision. He quickly ignored it and entered the room. Before making his way down to the lab, he remembered the keyboard he had flung across the room several days prior.

He unplugged the one from the computer he had never used in his immaculate showroom-like office. With the keyboard under his arm, he made his way down the elevator and into his lab, closing the heavy metal door behind him. He let out a loud sigh of relief as the humming from the cryogenic pod soothed his soul. He hobbled over to his computer and placed the keyboard on his desk before taking a seat. He sat there for several minutes letting his mind settle a little after the social interactions with Rita and Peter. He turned the computer on and listened back to the recording from his initial log, as if he was hearing all the words for the first time. After he was done, he stood up using his cane and grabbed a dewar flask, which he filled with the liquid nitrogen that he had been preparing next to Mary's cryogenic pod. He poured the contents into the opening of the machine, which he needed to upkeep to ensure it remained at the optimum temperature of -130°C. He then hobbled back to the computer and plugged in the new keyboard.

"Computer"

beep

"Record log."

"Log 2 – Project 808 – Recording."

beep

...

Project #: *808*
Encrypted Log Entry: *2*
Date & Time*: September 10, 2014, 11:17*
Log:

*808... That door... of course. We didn't even notice the project number when we first started this, but apparently our subconscious did. We had a nightmare, no... a vision. It seemed like a summary of our state of mind at the time as all nightmares and dreams are, but it felt ... like reality in every way. There's a deep thirst that is brewing within us, it feels like drug withdrawal. We **must** experience that world again. We **must** see her again, that place, despite how disturbing it was, is where we feel she is... it cannot be explained, we just know. That was the closest we've felt to Mary since she left this world, temporarily, it must be possible to interact with her again in our mind while we make progress towards reviving her.*

Regarding project 808, there are three areas we need to focus on:

   1. *Find a way to cure Mary's cancer, Adenocarcinomas. This is vital for her prolonged revival. It will require immense research, but*

we're confident we can achieve this.

2. *Reverse the death signal in her body. A current impossibility. Understanding death is a key requirement to reverse engineer it. Life wants to survive, so again, I'm-**we're** confident this is possible.*
3. *Create a form of hallucinogenic drug that will allow us to easily initiate and interact with these visions. A temporary solution to our sanity until we're able to make progress.*

This isn't going to be a quick process, we expect a few months at best if we dedicate all of our time and resources to this project. Let's hope our body doesn't let us down before we reach our goal. While Mary is safe in that pod for a long time, our body is the one running out of time. Once she's revived, we will look at a way to fix our own body.

"Computer, end recording."

beep

Unfortunately for Alexander, this was the beginning of a very long and painful journey spanning sixteen months of agonising research and spending. His old daily routines had returned to him, but without Mary by his side. Curing Adenocarcinomas was taking a significant amount of time, much longer than he had hoped in his pure arrogance, even with his now incredible understanding of the subject and all of the resources available to him through the secret society, Silver. Despite this, he was persistent and travelled all over the world visiting many different scientific institutions in pursuit of knowledge, working with the world's leading subject matter experts. During the long lonely road since Mary's death, he studied absolutely everything he could from the craziest of scientific theories to the most absurd supernatural fiction. Absolutely nothing was off the table, he investigated every single avenue and took them all seriously with blind faith despite his strong pride in the scientific method. He liaised with Lenny throughout the entire process, gathering as many instruments, chemicals and books as possible. While the cure was still outside of his grasp, he did have some success with his other two objectives. He made a major breakthrough with hallucinogenic and neural elixirs that targeted specific brain functions.

E1 – Targets the brain functions related to sleep and consciousness. This was crafted by Alexander in an attempt to perfectly lucid dream and recreate the vision he had over a year prior.

E2 – This was his biggest achievement, using this he believes with a bit of tweaking he could bring Mary's body back to life, reversing the death signal after thawing her out of cryosleep. It had the potential to reactivate all of the dormant cells in her body as long as there were still enough living cells to achieve Mitosis.

With how these elixirs were carefully crafted by Alexander in his lab, the ramifications of drinking them were completely unknown and potentially dangerous to human beings. The elixirs did however prove to have very convincing results on the unfortunate mice that he experimented on, but the question of human consumption remained. Despite all of the incredible success with the elixirs that could change humanity forever, he was deeply depressed. Throughout the sixteen months, he felt numb and detached from reality. He became more careless as his focus on making progress turned into an obsession. In the back of his mind he knew he was racing against Death itself so there was no time to be spent on lesser important things. His public appearance was far detached from how he behaved privately, to the point that they almost felt like entirely different people from radically different upbringings. His public appearance was kind, caring and chatty, and the other was a desperate, devious and depressed hermit. Worst of all, the stroke had seemingly left him with some memory loss, but it was very selective and short term, he'd sometimes not recall entire chunks of the previous day, totally relying on his recordings.

"Computer"
beep
"Record log."
"Log 231 – Project 808 – Recording."
beep

…

Project #: *808*
Encrypted Log Entry: *231*
Date & Time*: January 13, 2016, 13:11*
Log:

Dr. Abel in California wants to meet with us regarding Adenocarcinomas. He said he was touched by the magazine article which highlighted our goal to spend the remainder of our career on finding a cure in memory of Mary. He told us that he's made a breakthrough discovery and wishes to discuss it in person. Our jet leaves tomorrow morning.

"Computer, end recording." said Alexander in a grittier deeper tone.

beep

Alexander struggled to stand up from his computer, holding onto his cane carefully with a fragile and shaky grip. Over the course of the sixteen months, the after effects of the stroke sharply worsened and he had become much more frail. He had spent the last four months isolated deep in study and it showed physically, he had a long scruffy grey beard, his hair was an overgrown mess, his personal hygiene was almost non-existent and worse of all he was extremely emaciated, looking like skin and bones. Books were scattered throughout the lab, even covering the inflatable bed which laid in the corner not too far away from the cryogenic pod. Rotten fruit was overflowing out of the bin, which stank the lab out. This was a much different Alexander Lowe. He turned around from his computer and began manoeuvring through his cluttered and messy lab towards the pod which itself was pristine and well looked after. He began pouring the liquid nitrogen into the machine which he had upgraded several times, most notably to allow for more of the substance. This meant that

Alexander could leave Mary's body unattended while he went on longer trips across the world to further his research. Once he was done pouring the contents of the flask, he crawled onto the inflatable bed and curled up into the fetal position, immediately falling into a deep sleep.

IV

Alexander awoke to a high pitched alarm, his eyes were immediately violated by the artificial light emanating from the bright ceiling lights of the lab. He groaned to himself for a moment, trying to find the energy to match his desire to get up. He turned off the alarm on his wristwatch, and grabbed the passport that was waiting next to the bed.

He drove himself home and stared at the house for some time before finally plucking up the courage to enter it again. Since Mary's death, he had very rarely gone back home, usually only to shower before business trips. He quickly made his way to the same shower bath that still haunted him to this day. Every time he forced himself to wash, he'd see the water from the shower head replace itself with blood which would cover his body. The smell from that fateful day also manifested itself in his sinuses every time. He of course knew that this was his brain replaying the trauma but every time it happened, it startled him just as much as the first time he experienced it. He began shaving his long scruffy beard off and styled his grey hair to match his usual public appearance. To most people this was just a mundane daily task, but to this deeply depressed hermit, this felt like the worst kind of torture. When he was ready, he drove himself to the airport where he was escorted by two Silver henchmen to a private jet that he had organised through Lenny. To his surprise, the jet was surrounded by other henchmen wearing the same silvery vulture pin on their suits. The society, while shrouded in secrecy, was very bold as they had many influential clients in both the government and media, allowing them to move freely as long as they covered their tracks. The details of the organisation itself however, never left the mouths of those associated with it.

As he boarded the plane, Hubert was sitting down waiting for him with a very calculated look on his face. Hubert, as always, was dressed extremely well in a blue tailored suit, an expensive gold watch and confidence that radiated around him that mixed with the strong expensive cologne that hung in the air.

"Hubert? What are you doing here?" asked a puzzled Alexander.

"We need to talk." said Hubert as his cold blue eyes locked onto Alexander. He gestured at the seat in front of him.

"You're not one for face to face meetings with

clients, I don't think I've seen you in over ten years?" pondered Alexander while taking a seat.

"While I usually like to keep our chats brief, exclusive to the telephone, what I have to say needs to be said face to face, especially to a client of your tenure and with your previous experience working for us as a Shade." said Hubert, getting straight to the point.

An air steward came over, interrupting the discussion before it even began. She poured two glasses of champagne and placed them on their individual tables. Neither of them acknowledged her, and were staring at each other in a tense and silent stand-off. Alexander broke the gaze and picked up the champagne glass.

"Go on…" said Alexander while looking at the bubbles in the champagne.

"You're broke."

The tension rose, Alexander looked up at Hubert in confusion.

"Excuse me?"

"You have exactly £11,712 left in your bank account as of this morning."

"That is *impossible*," said Alexander abruptly.

"Is it?" snapped Hubert as he signalled to one of the henchmen standing next to them. He passed Alexander a tablet that was logged into his private bank account.

"How long did you think your wild spending was going to last? You've spent just shy of £9,000,000 in the last year alone."

"Nine, **million**?" asked Alexander, absolutely shocked by the figure and what he was seeing on the tablet.

"Your current income from your government job, your previous pay from the society, your lifelong savings and miscellaneous ventures is tremendous but even all of that couldn't cover your ridiculous spending."

Alexander knew he had to be careful with what he told Hubert, he couldn't tell him the truth but he couldn't lie to him either. Hubert was a fiscal and operational mastermind whose aura demanded respect and honesty, he would easily smell any deception on the words leaving Alexander's tongue.

"My Silver services are-"

Hubert immediately raised his finger at the word 'Silver', silencing Alexander.

"Apologies, it's been some time. I understand that the services provided by the society must be paid for. Have I ever missed one of the yearly payments in the last thirty years?"

Hubert continued to stare at Alexander, only raising an eyebrow slightly to confirm he had indeed never missed a payment.

"Hubert, the upcoming payment in February will be no different. As I'm sure you're aware, I've been working on something huge which will make me a lot of money. Everything that I've spent over the last sixteen months has been invested into this." said Alexander as he began to sweat.

Hubert leaned forward very slowly as his eyes narrowed.

"Alexander, I need you to know that even with your history with our group… if a payment is missed, you will forfeit all of our services forever, permanently, and you will never see me, Lenny or anyone else from our world ever again. Once the switch is flicked, all of our shadows will vanish."

"The projec-" said Alexander before being interrupted once again.

"Alexander, you should know better. I promise, I really do not care about your ventures. What you do with your money, your time or anything we provide to you is never any of our concern and it never will be. We are not friends, we are acquaintances and that's how it will always remain unless a payment is missed." said Hubert, sitting back in his chair before downing the entire champagne glass.

"I understand." acknowledged a defeated Alexander.

Hubert stood up with his eyes still locked on Alexander while buttoning up his suit.

"Consider this flight a gift from me personally, you couldn't have afforded it anyway. It's only one way so you'll need to figure out how to get back to the UK." said Hubert before he and his men abruptly made their way out of the jet, leaving only his champagne glass behind.

After landing in California, Alexander made his way to the Cancer Treatment and Research Laboratory where he hobbled his way into the reception area using his trusty cane.

"Hello, I'm here to see Dr. Abel."

"Ah, Dr. Lowe? He's been expecting you. Please, take a seat, I'll call him down to collect you. Could you sign in for me please?"

Alexander signed his name, time of arrival and his signature. As he was going to sit down, his attention was caught by the paintings on the wall. He walked closer to the artwork and began to read the notes next to them. The paintings were all done by local artists specifically for the research lab. As he admired the paintings fondly, he couldn't ignore his thoughts any longer, this was potentially the breakthrough that he needed and it couldn't have come at a better time, especially with the news that

Hubert delivered to him personally. The enthusiasm in Dr. Abel's voice on the phone was nothing like any of the other interactions Alexander had in the past sixteen months which all turned out to be dead ends.

"Alex?" asked a voice which broke his gaze away from the paintings.

Alexander looked around to find a tall dark haired man standing before him with a big smile on his face. He was well dressed, and donned a pristine white lab coat over his beige clothing "It's a pleasure to finally meet you in person." he continued.

Alexander smiled, "The pleasure is all mine, Dr. Abel."

Dr. Abel immediately noticed how frail he looked compared to the previous media appearances he saw Alexander participate in. He extended his hand out, which exposed a colourful pink and yellow handmade bracelet. Alexander shook his hand as firmly as he could in a show of mutual respect.

"Please, call me Steve." he said with a sudden concern in his face as he noticed Alexander's weak grip "Come with me, we have *a lot* to discuss," he said as he put his hand on Alexander's back in a comforting and friendly gesture.

As they made their way up the elevator, Steven could

not shake his thoughts about the state that Alexander was in.

"I just wanted to say that I'm so sorry for your loss last year, Alex. I can't imagine what you've been through."

Alexander lowered his head slightly. He knew that he was at the end of his rope, and it was pointless bottling it up anymore. He decided to lower his defences and allow his vulnerabilities to show, feeling a sense of trust in Steven.

"I wouldn't wish this dread upon anyone, Steve. It's been hell." said Alexander, staring forwards at the elevator screen, waiting for it to stop.

Steven nodded, not saying anything for a few moments until the elevator reached the eighth floor.

"Hopefully what I have to show you will make you very pleased. I'm actually very excited to see your reaction."

The elevator let out a loud beep which prompted Steven to swipe his ID card on the door. Alexander's jaw dropped as he looked upon the beautiful lab which opened up in front of him, it was kitted out with the most modern equipment on the market today, things that would make any scientist envious. As Alexander's mind began spending money he didn't have, his eyes were drawn to a large portable whiteboard with notes and equations scribbled all over it in the centre of the room.

"What is that?" enquired Alexander, pointing at it.

Steven smiled and folded his arms in pride as Alexander eagerly hobbled his way over to it.

"That, my friend, will be the cure to Adenocarcinomas."

Alexander stopped in his tracks before reaching the whiteboard and chuckled to himself in disbelief, completely out of character. Steven leaned against a column in the room, smiling confidently and saying nothing further. Alexander adjusted his glasses and began analysing it carefully. He fell silent for several minutes, his eyes were frantically darting all around the whiteboard as his brain was processing it all at lightning speed.

...

"*This is it*... This is what I've been searching for..." he said, putting the palm of his hand on an empty space on the whiteboard "No... actually... this isn't a cure for Adenocarcinomas." he continued, taking a step back "This is something **far** greater, this would be revolutionary." he said as his eyes widened in disbelief as serotonin began pumping around his brain wildly.

The notes on the whiteboard made no reference to Adenocarcinomas, but there was no need. The equations and notes showed quite clearly a way to expand far beyond anything currently possible in modern medicine, to even call it modern medicine wouldn't do it justice. This was a brand new avenue of science, some of it didn't even make sense to Alexander as if he was reading an evolved form of scientific notation. It was **BEAUTIFUL**.

"A cure that can be programmed… for anything…?" said Alexander under his breath.

"Alex, we can save Mary with this..."

Alexander snapped out of his awe, turning to Steven in shock at what he just said. How could he possibly know about his intent to revive Mary?

"E-excuse me?" asked Alexander as his heart began pounding violently.

"I said we can save so many with this."

Alexander immediately calmed down, clearly mishearing him.

"This is incredible. Do… Do you realise what this means? You'll save millions… no… **BILLIONS!**"

"My team spent the last twenty years working on this. I mean, we can't take all the credit, we built this on the shoulders of giants that came before us of course, but my team worked tirelessly to get us to this point, especially over the last year." confirmed Steven who was now standing next to him, smiling proudly at the whiteboard.

Alexander hadn't cried in over a year, but he couldn't control the flow of tears that began pouring down his cheeks. The old Alexander had finally resurfaced once again. This was not only incredible news, but it was just ... ***beautiful***. The feeling in his stomach, it was not something he had felt since he first fell in love with science as a young boy and not only that, his journey was finally over. He now had everything he needed to save Mary's life and revive her.

"How is it administered?" asked Alexander suddenly, changing his tone. He began pacing around the whiteboard like a boy in a sweet shop.

"That's the thing, once we program the nanobots to adhere to our instructions, it's just a matter of getting them into the bloodstream, a simple injection, or even a pill would suffice."

"Nanobots?" asked Alexander in disbelief. This was all future tech that he never expected to see in his lifetime, or so he thought "Incredible..." he muttered in astonishment.

"Welcome to a new world of medicine where every treatment is custom made. We haven't found a single thing we couldn't cure during our trials. Cancer, blindness, heart disease, dementia, Alzheimer's, it doesn't matter... and the best part? It will likely cost pennies when it's mass produced." continued Steven.

Alexander was stunned at the words coming out of Steve's mouth, if successful, this could have the potential to cure anything.

They spent the next few hours exchanging ideas, wisdom, past times and even how they became interested in science at an early age. The conversation eventually turned to the inevitable, the miracle medicine and how it was produced.

"The cure that the patient requires is carefully programmed by artificial intelligence in a matter of minutes, this ensures that it is fully compatible with the genetic makeup of the patient. The nanobots are then wirelessly passed this information, and are all programmed to carry out very specific tasks. The nanobots are then put inside a pill, which when swallowed, enters the patient's stomach, where the outer coating dissolves, like any other pill. Upon contact with the stomach fluids, the pill is broken down and the bots travel to the small intestines to be absorbed along with the other nutrients. Once in the bloodstream, they activate. They will then begin to wirelessly communicate with one another, organising themselves and spreading out through the body. Each one then begins completing their respective tasks until the patient is fully healed."

"This is just incredible, Steve. How many of you have been working on this?"

"It's just my team, we are reluctant to divulge too much as we know how thirsty those medical companies are. As soon as they get a whiff of this, they'll find a way to get their grubby hands on it and charge a thousand times the cost to produce."

"That makes sense, I know all too well how that world operates." said Alexander in agreement.

"As I said earlier, we stand on the shoulders of giants in our field, but we have also learnt from their mistakes. Keeping our mouths shut is the best approach for something as important as this. The fact is, this can be mass produced very easily, and it's extremely affordable. We're talking about a few dollars, or pounds in your currency, to produce per patient. The only other person, other than yourself, is Dr. Woodfine. He has been a great help to our team, he's an unknown, but he's the mastermind behind the nanobots and their AI. A modern genius, like yourself!"

"You are too kind, Steve."

Alexander was completely enthralled by the research, and captivated at what it could mean for Mary's revival. Not only that, this was the first **real** positive interaction he had since waking up that fateful day in August 2014. A familiar beep was suddenly heard coming from the other side of the lab.

"Locking up time boys!" shouted a security guard entering the lab briefly from the elevator.

"Ah crap, it's 8pm. My wife is going to kill me." laughed Steven.

Alexander laughed along and stood himself up with his cane, much quicker than usual with his newfound energy and optimism.

"Do you think you could synthesise it for me, and program it so it could cure Adenocarcinomas?"

Steven glanced at Alexander, confused.

"I'd love to analyse it myself in my own lab using my equipment. If that's okay with you?" continued Alexander.

The concern in Steven's face faded.

"Oh of course. I don't see why not as long as it stays in your lab and **strictly** between us. We'll be sharing our research publicly in a few months anyway if all goes well. I'll have to make you sign an NDA of course, sorry, company policy. This is strictly confidential for now until we're ready to publish our papers to the scientific community. But yes, absolutely, we can make a few batches for you."

"That would be great, thank you Steve."

Steven smiled, and then once again looked over Alexander's frail body with concern.

"Say, how would you like to stay at our place during your visit to Cali? My wife would love to meet you, she's a bigger geek than I am if you could imagine. She's an incredible cook too, so she'd feed you well!"

The gesture took Alexander by surprise, this was such an abnormal thought for him, and he had planned to book a flight home as soon as possible. His inner demons began rising back to the surface, which were persuading him to get home and hermit himself in his lab. In a completely autonomous movement, he placed his hand on his other arm, instantly relaxing himself.

"That would be lovely." said Alexander with a little excitement in his voice.

Alexander stayed at Dr. Abel's home with his wife and daughter. He knew that he deserved some time to finally relax and be around a positive environment especially after everything he had been through. The days turned into a week, and Alexander was filled with positive vibes which knocked him out of his tunnel vision, allowing his soul to be somewhat soothed before the long journey home. Steven could see a huge difference in Alexander's demeanour and health throughout his time at their home, and it was very encouraging.

"Do you have a wife, Xander?" asked Steven's daughter, struggling to say Alexander's name.

"Katie, hey." said Steven, gently pulling her over to himself "What have I told you about being so direct with people?"

"Oh sorry! I just saw his ring!" she said eagerly while pointing.

Alexander looked at the ring on his finger, he had almost forgotten it was there because it had been a part of him for so long.

"It's okay Katie, it's good to be curious and inquisitive. I do indeed have a wife, her name is Mary." said Alexander, smiling briefly at Steven in understanding.

"Is she pretty?"

"She's the most beautiful woman in the world, although I'm sure she might have some competition when you're much much older!" joked Alexander.

Katie giggled.

"Where is she?"

Steven tugged on her once again.

"Katie…"

"She's currently sleeping, she's actually been asleep for a long time…"

"She's a lazybones! My dad calls me lazybones when I sleep too much!" she giggled.

Alexander laughed.

"Well, she'll be awake again soon enough, I'm sure." said Alexander, as his eyes darted to Steven, then back at Katie.

"Does she like bracelets? I really love making bracelets, I've made lots of them, you know?"

Alexander looked at the bright and colourful bracelets on her wrists, which had the same sort of design as the one he saw on Steven's wrist when they first met.

"These are very well made, Katie, maybe someday you can be an Engineer?"

Steven's wife heard the comment as she was entering the room and chuckled.

"With how often she breaks things around here, she'd be an Engineer's worst nightmare."

Later that night, Alexander and Steven were on the roof terrace of the family home, drinking wine and admiring the stars.

"You have a beautiful family, Steve. And your home is incredible."

"I'm a very lucky man, Alex, I count my blessings every single day."

"This new avenue of medicine you're about to unleash on the world is going to change everything. I hope you realise the magnitude of your team's accomplishment? It might be the biggest advancement in the history of mankind ever. Your child's generation might be living young and healthy for centuries."

"That's why we're being extra cautious with who we're sharing our research with until we're secure. It's **essential** that this isn't privatised, as it **must** be accessible to everyone. This is humanity's best chance at long term survival regardless of social status. Imagine a world where only rich annoying celebrities are around forever." joked Steven "No offence!" he laughed further.

Alexander laughed along.

"I am still sometimes bewildered at my celebrity status. I'm not entirely sure why people find my work interesting."

"Well, as a fan myself, I can tell you. Your research is very interesting, and all those old interviews you used to do on TV were really accessible to even children, you were a man of the people, that's for sure. I mean, you still are, of course."

"It's been a long time since I was in the spotlight, before Mary's illness."

"You can still be that person, even after her death,

Alex. It's just going to take time."

"Yes, I am fairly confident that things will improve very soon, Steve."

They toasted each other.

Early the next morning, Steven made a batch of his programmable cure, specifically aimed at curing Adenocarcinomas. He showed Alexander how it could be programmed to a specific patient's body using some specialist equipment that Alexander would have to find a way to purchase with the remainder of his limited funds.

Later on, Alexander waved off his new friends at the drop off and made his way through the airport to his less glamorous economy flight home to London. While waiting for the flight, he made a call to Lenny and ordered the equipment which was to be delivered to the lab the next morning. Alexander knew that this would put him into the red, but it didn't matter anymore. The deep depression he had a week prior had lifted, and his overall health felt much better than it had in a long time. On the flight home, he began writing up extensive plans for how he was going to revive Mary, and any mitigations for any potential problems that might present themselves. Before he knew it, the plane was landing in London. He picked up his checked in luggage, which contained the miracle new medicine that would play a crucial part in Mary's revival. He was gleaming with confidence and joy, even sleeping in his own bed like a baby when he arrived back home, knowing that he'd be waking up next to Mary once again in the same bed very soon.

Alexander awoke. The sun was gleaming off every reflective surface of the room, filling it with light. He looked at the empty side of the bed, not with sadness but with excitement. Today was finally the day. He looked at the clock, which read 09:30am, a good omen for things to come. He quickly got himself ready and drove his way to the lab, holding the satchel containing the cure close to his side. He picked up the delivered equipment with his portable dolly and made his way into his office as the door automatically locked behind him. He moved the bookcase to the side, unlocked the metal door in front of him and pulled the string that controlled the lights.

…

Nothing.

…

He tried again…

...

The light did not turn on. He walked over to the light switch in the office itself, and it turned on without a problem. He hobbled back over to the dimly lit elevator and breathed in nervously before pressing the red button that controlled the elevator.

...

Again, nothing.

...

He tried again with more force, ***nothing.***

"No..." said Alexander under his breath as his body began shivering, knowing the potential consequences of what this might mean, especially if the light in the office itself was working.

He kept pressing the button repeatedly, hoping it was just jammed, but nothing happened. As his button presses became more erratic, the elevator creaked and roared down the shaft below him at the slightest movement. Feeling panicked, he quickly grabbed the elevator mechanisms, moving the gears manually himself with his hands, which

"SHE IS GONE, **SHE IS GONE!**"

"I must... Maybe... no... fuck **FUCK!** THERE'S NOTHING! **NOTHING LEFT!**"

He began feeling for the circuit breakers on the wall again like a rabid animal smashing into anything that got in his way. Eventually he found them and turned the lights back on. He quickly rushed over to where his elixirs and other chemicals were, grabbed any full test tube he could find and drank them all without a second thought. This was the end and the cocktail of chemicals travelling down his oesophagus confirmed that fate. He began seeing things, figures, her body, psychedelic shapes, as his brain felt like it was smashing to pieces. He paced back over to the cryogenic pod, with a lake of tears pouring down his face and put his hand on Mary's badly decomposed arm. The slime that came off her arm startled him at first but he quickly ignored it.

"I'll ... see ... you soon, my love-ly." whimpered a hysterical Alexander, rubbing her arm as she always did with him.

He closed his eyes, awaiting his fate as the illusions turned to nausea.

"don't... do... this... Alexander... *PLEASE!*" echoed Mary's words inside his brain.

The hairs on his arms rose, goosebumps erupted all

over the back of his neck and a tingle shot down his spine like lightning. He opened his eyes and saw a silhouette in the shape of Mary briefly. He began to feel deep regret as something powerful was stirring in his mind from the same unknown origin that had been comforting him in Mary's absence whenever he was hysterical. This was different though, her voice was as clear as it had ever been. He looked all around the room but saw no sign of his beloved wife, no silhouette, no shapes, just him, alone which triggered a feeling of extreme loneliness in that moment. His eyes widened in disbelief, he knew she was still there somehow, he could feel it, he just couldn't see her. He put his fingers in his throat and made himself throw up all over the floor of the lab, which took the majority of the chemicals out of his stomach before they could be absorbed into his body. He stumbled over to the machine and placed his hand on the power switch with his quaking hands. He knew that what was in front of him was no longer Mary, she must be... something else, somewhere else. The machine was no longer serving any purpose other than tripping the power. He looked down at her corpse in a psychotic gaze trying to regain his composure but it was a failing effort.

"I'm so, so sorry for what I put you through. I hope you understand why I did it? You did right? Talk to me again. I need to hear your voice."

No comforting words came as he had hoped.

"I wish I was some dumb piece of shit so I didn't have to carry this burden of responsibility on my back. The fact is Mary, I was *SO* close to reviving you. I could've done it. **I WAS SO CLOSE!**" he said with tears continuing to erupt down his cheeks "I could've done it... You have no idea. I can't go on. Please don't make me. Let me be with you instead, wherever you are." he said, looking again at the chemicals in the corner of the room.

He once again put his hand on his arm autonomously, which caused him to gasp.

"M-mary?! That was you, right?" he asked out loud in surprise while looking around.

"No, but you *must* go on."

This voice was male and unfamiliar, which startled him. It echoed from deep within his own mind which was very unsettling. It was calm, and seemed to have multiple layers to it, almost like a silky growl.

...

"I can't, I'm not strong enough for this fight anymore." said Alexander out loud.

"*You* aren't, but *I* am."

...

"Let... *me*."

...

"*okay...*" replied Alexander softly under his breath.

● ● ●

Alexander felt a wash of painful cold air blast over his head. His eyes began twitching as if his brain was seemingly being reprogrammed. His soul, his very essence was being shattered and he felt every single part of it crumbling away into the depths, but he did not fight it, instead he welcomed the pain which he saw as a punishment for what he had done. His pupils dilated and his demeanour immediately changed to a much calmer, fully alert Alexander. The room fell silent once again.

...

very slowly descended him down into the depths towards the lab. This took a significant amount of time and Alexander's hands were badly cut up from the sharp rusty gears. He finally heard the familiar but less audible clank as it reached the bottom. Other than the dim light above him from the office, he was completely blind. He held onto the wall and used his cane to feel around his surroundings. He heard the thump of metal in front of him, recognising it as the entrance to the lab. He fumbled around and eventually found the string for the light. He pulled it.

Nothing.

"No no no no... **FUCK!**" he shouted, which echoed up the elevator shaft.

He frantically grabbed his keys from his pocket but dropped them onto the floor. He bent down to feel where he thought they landed, but instead whacked his head into the metal door in the process.

"**FUCK!**" he shouted again angrily.

He finally found his keys using his bloodied hands, and eventually located the lock. He inserted the key, turned it, unlocked it and shoulder barged the door open. After barging in, his cane fell to the floor somewhere behind him. After the noise of the cane falling ceased, the room was eerily silent, something he hadn't heard in well over a year with the constant humming of the cryogenic pod, which was no longer present.

"No no no… **Please…**"

The pain from not using his cane was excruciating, but the adrenaline pumping around his body was pushing it aside. He eventually found the circuit breaker near the door using his hands. He lifted the cover and felt that the switch was down. He flipped it back up, but once again, nothing happened. Alexander then quickly remembered the backup circuit breaker he had installed next to it several months prior and did the same to that one, which this time lit up the lab and the elevator shaft. The light was overwhelming, so he shielded his eyes briefly before quickly limping over to the cryogenic pod. He put his hands on the glass panel, which was thick with condensation.

…

It was room temperature.

…

"*no…*" he whimpered under his breath as his heart rate rose even higher, which was deafening in the silent lab.

In a blind intense panic he pulled open the machine but before he could see inside, a thick unpleasant smell hit him in the face, it was like nothing he had ever experienced before, his eyes instinctively closed and his entire body jolted back. He forced his eyes open.

...

Lying before him was Mary's badly decomposed remains.

...

It was over. This was the end of the road. Not only that, it had clearly been over for quite some time, likely right after he left for the airport. Every breath he took felt like his face was being covered by a damp rag soaked in rotten meat, which stung his nostrils.

...

Alexander's machine gun heartbeat was suddenly interrupted by the hum of the cryogenic pod which had started itself up again automatically. This triggered the power to trip, sending the room into darkness once again.

...

Silence, total and absolute.

...

Suddenly blood curdling screams began echoing throughout the pitch black lab as Alexander started smashing everything within arms reach, including the satchel holding Dr. Abel's programmable cure. He embraced the darkness around him, using it to only strengthen the manifestation of his emotions like a masquerade mask, this was the end of not only Mary's life but Alexander's as well, and he knew it. The image of Mary's body was blinding despite the room being pitch black.

"*NO!*" screamed a crazed Alexander, as he began pacing through the void of his lab, knocking into everything.

He began to quickly lose his mind, whispering nonsense to himself.

"Why? Mary? How could this... are you?"

"No, I can... wait... so... no... No NO **NO!**"

"She's gone but... no... I could... no? No! She's gone."

"She's gone."

"SHE IS GONE, **SHE IS GONE!**"

"I must... Maybe... no... fuck **FUCK!** THERE'S NOTHING! **NOTHING LEFT!**"

He began feeling for the circuit breakers on the wall again like a rabid animal smashing into anything that got in his way. Eventually he found them and turned the lights back on. He quickly rushed over to where his elixirs and other chemicals were, grabbed any full test tube he could find and drank them all without a second thought. This was the end and the cocktail of chemicals travelling down his oesophagus confirmed that fate. He began seeing things, figures, her body, psychedelic shapes, as his brain felt like it was smashing to pieces. He paced back over to the cryogenic pod, with a lake of tears pouring down his face and put his hand on Mary's badly decomposed arm. The slime that came off her arm startled him at first but he quickly ignored it.

"I'll ... see ... you soon, my love-ly." whimpered a hysterical Alexander, rubbing her arm as she always did with him.

He closed his eyes, awaiting his fate as the illusions turned to nausea.

"don't... do... this... Alexander... ***PLEASE!***" echoed Mary's words inside his brain.

The hairs on his arms rose, goosebumps erupted all

over the back of his neck and a tingle shot down his spine like lightning. He opened his eyes and saw a silhouette in the shape of Mary briefly. He began to feel deep regret as something powerful was stirring in his mind from the same unknown origin that had been comforting him in Mary's absence whenever he was hysterical. This was different though, her voice was as clear as it had ever been. He looked all around the room but saw no sign of his beloved wife, no silhouette, no shapes, just him, alone which triggered a feeling of extreme loneliness in that moment. His eyes widened in disbelief, he knew she was still there somehow, he could feel it, he just couldn't see her. He put his fingers in his throat and made himself throw up all over the floor of the lab, which took the majority of the chemicals out of his stomach before they could be absorbed into his body. He stumbled over to the machine and placed his hand on the power switch with his quaking hands. He knew that what was in front of him was no longer Mary, she must be... something else, somewhere else. The machine was no longer serving any purpose other than tripping the power. He looked down at her corpse in a psychotic gaze trying to regain his composure but it was a failing effort.

"I'm so, so sorry for what I put you through. I hope you understand why I did it? You did right? Talk to me again. I need to hear your voice."

No comforting words came as he had hoped.

"I wish I was some dumb piece of shit so I didn't have to carry this burden of responsibility on my back. The fact is Mary, I was *SO* close to reviving you. I could've done it. **I WAS SO CLOSE!**" he said with tears continuing to erupt down his cheeks "I could've done it… You have no idea. I can't go on. Please don't make me. Let me be with you instead, wherever you are." he said, looking again at the chemicals in the corner of the room.

He once again put his hand on his arm autonomously, which caused him to gasp.

"M-mary?! That was you, right?" he asked out loud in surprise while looking around.

"No, but you *must* go on."

This voice was male and unfamiliar, which startled him. It echoed from deep within his own mind which was very unsettling. It was calm, and seemed to have multiple layers to it, almost like a silky growl.

…

"I can't, I'm not strong enough for this fight anymore." said Alexander out loud.

"*You* aren't, but *I* am."

...

"Let... *me*."

...

"*okay...*" replied Alexander softly under his breath.

● ● ●

Alexander felt a wash of painful cold air blast over his head. His eyes began twitching as if his brain was seemingly being reprogrammed. His soul, his very essence was being shattered and he felt every single part of it crumbling away into the depths, but he did not fight it, instead he welcomed the pain which he saw as a punishment for what he had done. His pupils dilated and his demeanour immediately changed to a much calmer, fully alert Alexander. The room fell silent once again.

...

He breathed in deeply, and exhaled slowly, letting out a soft bassy growl from the depths of his lungs.

...

He looked around the room as if he was seeing it properly for the first time, analysing his bloodied cut hands closely. He looked at the breakers on the wall, piecing together what had just transpired. He looked back at the cryogenic pod and immediately powered it off for good. His eyes slowly shifted to Mary's horrifically decomposed body, but he showed no sign of emotion. He began pacing over to the other side of the lab but he was quickly overcome with severe pain in his left leg, to his surprise.

"*So weak...*" he said to himself disappointedly under his breath at his limitations.

He continued on and grabbed the body bag that Lenny's henchmen had brought her in prior, putting her into it and zipping it up without a care. As the clock struck midnight, he left the now empty premises and threw the body into his car, not even acknowledging the pungent smell coming from the bag. He drove to a nearby nature reserve, where he spent the night digging up a grave deep in the foliage. He removed her from the car and dropped the body bag down to the edge of the grave before finally pushing her into the deep hole using his foot. He spent the remainder of the night covering the body with the soil that he had dug up. As he finished, the sun was beginning to rise. He drove back home and stumbled into the bathroom, looking at himself in the mirror with curiosity, examining each crevice of his face with the same dilated pupils.

"***Such fragility…***" he growled to himself.

He stared at his hair which left him dumbfounded. He quickly began shaving his head bald without a second thought. He then took a long hot shower, no longer seeing the mental images of blood spraying from it anymore. He put on a freshly ironed white shirt, secured it with a blue tie, pulled up his khaki trousers and finally covered himself with his white lab coat which was now a little too large for him to his surprise. He got into his car and made his way to work, where he was the first to arrive. He took a seat on the steps leading up to the entrance of the building and began staring at the car park entrance, watching the cars entering one by one. As the hours passed by, different members of staff walked by him on the stairs, but they didn't recognise him. They all continued into the building until Rita took a second glance.

"Alex? Is that you? It is, isn't it?"

Alexander didn't respond. He kept his focus on the

car park entrance like a lion waiting for its prey.

"I'm digging the new look." she said, but no reply came.

...

"Are you okay?"

"Go inside," said Alexander harshly in a deeper and gritter tone that she had never heard from him before.

Rita kneeled down to him with concern.

"You're not okay. What's wrong? Did something happen?"

As Rita asked the question, Alexander's eyes began tracking a red car entering the car park. He stood himself up with his cane and paced towards it as it parked up. Peter, who had recently just parked himself a few moments beforehand, walked up the stairs and met Rita who was watching Alexander hobble away.

"What's going on?" asked a puzzled Peter.

"I have no idea. I think he's going towards Francis's car?" questioned Rita, trying to understand the situation herself.

"Maybe he's finally giving him his marching orders? Long overdue." laughed Peter.

Rita continued to watch on in concern.

Francis leaned over to the back seat of his car and grabbed his plastic bag full of food and drinks for the week. Alexander opened the car door with great force, hitting it against the lamppost next to the car. Francis jumped in his seat at the suddenness of the movement and the loud noise.

"What the fuck? You scared the shit out of me you idiot!" barked Francis.

"My office, go. *Now.*" said Alexander venomously before walking off and leaving the car door open.

Francis immediately changed his demeanour after vaguely recognising Alexander.

"Hey, hold up a sec, I'm on time! What's this about?" shouted Francis from his car, but Alexander had already stumbled back halfway between the car park and the main entrance. He passed by Peter and Rita and made his way to his office.

Francis threw the unlocked door open in anger. This was the first time he had been inside Alexander's showroom-like office. He was greeted by Alexander who was sitting behind his desk.

"Well?! What's all this about?" demanded Francis, throwing his arms outwards in frustration.

Alexander did not answer, instead he waited for the door to lock itself automatically behind Francis, which startled him during the silent standoff.

"Sit." instructed Alexander, motioning to the chair in front of him.

Francis walked over to the desk.

"Look mate, I'm not late, I arrived on time like everyone else. How about we talk about you paying for the damage to my car door!"

Alexander kept staring at Francis, waiting for him to comply with his instruction.

"Well?!" shouted Francis, trying to control the conversation. He stared intensely at Alexander, but his cold dilated pupils showed no sign of emotion.

Francis began to feel uneasy at Alexander's demeanour.

"Look... I... I don't have time for this, I have shit to do." said Francis as he attempted to open the door, but it didn't budge "Hey..." he attempted again "Unlock the door!" demanded Francis.

"**Sit. Down.**" instructed Alexander in a more sinister tone, watching Francis's mannerisms closely.

"You know you can't lock me in here against my will, right? It's against the law."

"You don't want to hear the good news?" asked Alexander.

"What good news?" asked Francis while still holding

onto the door handle.

Alexander's emotionless face manifested into a slight grin.

"You may have noticed that I have been quite preoccupied over the last year and a half. I have been working with a colleague in California who has created something quite remarkable. Something that will revolutionise medicine and by extension, the world."

"Okay…?" replied Francis dumbfounded, still holding onto the door handle.

"They would like our help, and I will need a team manager." Alexander gestured his hand to Francis "I am promoting you."

Francis shook his head in disbelief, cracking a smile. His ego put everything else that was happening aside, focusing entirely on this unexpected positive news. He immediately knew that this might be his big opportunity.

"Oh… wow, really? That's… that's great news! T-thank you!" said both a surprised and excited Francis. He let go of the door handle and faced Alexander.

Alexander stood up, offering his hand to Francis, who immediately shook it. Francis's attention was caught by the deep cuts on Alexander's hands, which had not healed from the elevator gears the previous day.

"Congratulations." said Alexander as he squeezed his

hand tightly, eyeing him up as if he was a three course meal. Francis was too self absorbed in his own thoughts to notice the red flags that were beginning to rise up all around him.

"What is it I'll be working on?" asked Francis with curiosity.

"How about I show you a prototype? I think you will be quite impressed." said Alexander as he turned to his bookcase, unclipping the mechanism and moving it to the side revealing the hidden door to the elevator.

"No way…" chuckled Francis "You've got to be kidding me, right? You seriously have a secret room behind a bookshelf?"

Alexander, unamused, motioned him to come over as he rattled the keys in his pocket with the other hand. Francis complied and stood beside him, eagerly awaiting entry to this secret room. Francis's mind began racing at the possibilities of being a team manager and the power over the others that this would give him, something he had been thirsting for his entire career at the lab. This would also be something that he could proudly share on his already inflated resumé that he could actually back up with merit. As Francis was daydreaming, Alexander calmly pushed a previously concealed syringe deep into Francis's thigh. He quickly jolted backwards, stumbling over

Alexander's desk.

"What the fuck?!" screamed Francis in disbelief.

Alexander turned towards him, with a sadistic smile.

"Is something the matter?"

"What did you just stab into my leg?!" he shouted again, while checking his thigh.

"You pathetic little lab rat." said Alexander with a slight chuckle "Do not worry" he said, lifting up the syringe into view "It's just a little something I cooked up, *it* won't kill you, but *I will*." he continued, carefully laying the syringe down on the bookshelf behind him.

Francis lunged over the desk but his strength was diminishing rapidly, he grabbed Alexander by the collar of his lab coat and began to feebly strike him. Alexander stood perfectly still and absorbed the cushioned punches. Francis was already far too under the influence of the contents of the syringe for him to be any form of threat. He frantically turned his attention to the office door again and began to barge into it with no effect.

"SOMEONE HELP ME!" screamed Francis at the top of his lungs as he attempted to pull at the door handle.

"If *I* were in your situation, I wouldn't expend my energy. These walls will only absorb your screams." said Alexander calmly, taking a seat again, neatening his desk to how it was before Francis had barged into it "*Sleep.*"

instructed Alexander.

Francis began to lose consciousness, sliding against the door down to the floor. Once Alexander was done tidying his desk, he looked over at Francis, seeing that he was now ready. He stood up, brushed himself off and walked over to Francis. Using a frighteningly strong grip from an unknown origin, he grabbed him and dragged his body behind the bookcase into the dark void like a lion hoarding its prey.

Francis woke up in a panicked daze. Migraine-like auras were overwhelming his vision and a splitting headache like one he had never experienced before was pulsating across his brain. As his vision cleared, he glanced around his surroundings, finding himself in a lab he had never seen before. The lights above him were blinding which triggered his migraine further, so he kept his eyes squinted, not wanting to aggravate the pounding feeling in his skull. He groggily looked down and to his horror he was tied to a chair with his hands behind his back. He finally noticed Alexander, who was sitting with his back to him distracted.

"W-what did you do to me? Where am I?" asked Francis.

"I dragged you down to my lab and I tied you up." replied Alexander as he was holding a test tube in his hand

and reading something on his monitor "I'm surprised you're already awake."

"Why have you done this to me?"

Alexander did not answer right away, deciding to finish what he was reading first.

"You're my first test subject." said Alexander calmly, in a darker tone.

"Test subject? For what?!"

Alexander chuckled to himself under his breath "You won't live long enough for that to matter to you…"

"WHAT! What have I done?!"

"I just like you the least." answered Alexander immediately while still distracted.

…

Francis's fears were confirmed, Alexander had lost his mind and he was about to become another statistic. He slumped forward in his chair avoiding the lights above him.

"Thank you." said Alexander, acknowledging Francis' silence, still looking at the monitor in front of him.

"Computer"

beep

"Record log."

"Log 232 – Project 808 – Recording."

beep

...

Project #: *808*
Encrypted Log Entry: *232*
Date & Time*: January 22, 2016, 13:34*
Log:

It's finally time to test these elixirs on a human subject. He is the pe-

SOMEONE HELP ME!

... He is the perfect subject for the E1 elixir.

No wife.

No children.

No life.

His family doesn't care about him.

He's rarely at work.

Everybody hates him.

Alex, PLEASE STOP. I'll do anything, PLEASE!

Nobody will miss this waste of oxygen once he's removed from reality.

ALEX!!!

*When you listen to this back, you may be wondering why you are continuing, and why you have done this. Rest assured, this is all part of **my** design, and **you** will see **her*** *again. Keep going, Alexander.*

"Computer, end recording." said Alexander.

beep

Alexander swivelled his chair around and stared at Francis in curiosity.

"I'm surprised you haven't asked what was in that injection I put into your thigh. Someone in your predicament should really be asking that question."

Francis raised his head in terror, his eyes finally widening "What... was in it?"

Alexander opened a drawer from the workbench and pulled out a boxcutter, checking the blade carefully to see if it was sharp or blunt.

"ALEX, NO! PLEASE STOP! DON'T DO THIS! **PLEASE!**" screamed a terrified Francis.

Alexander hobbled over and cut the cable ties around his wrists and ankles that were restraining him in place. Francis looked confused before gradually falling to his side, smacking his face into the cold hard ground. He groaned in pain.

"Why can't I... I- I can't move!" said Francis helplessly on the floor.

"That would make sense, I have paralysed you from the shoulders down-"

"W-"

"***Permanently***." interrupted Alexander with a sadistic grin on his face.

…

Francis began to sob hysterically, feeling completely vulnerable and helpless.

"Unfortunately, ***you*** will be the first human to fully experience this wonderful elixir created by my counterpart and I. I am actually a little jealous…" said Alexander, pausing for a moment "To set your mind at ease, 53% of the mice tested on survived, the others died from a heart attack after waking up, so the odds are ***slightly*** in your favour. I would very much like to avoid having to select another human subject with the limited time I have control over my body, so I would politely request that you not die yet until you have served your purpose."

Francis laid his head on the lab floor, praying to God to take him out of this nightmare. Alexander squatted next to him with the support of his cane.

"It's unfortunate that your tenure as Team Manager was cut short, this might be the last time we speak. So, before we begin, would you like to know a little secret?"

Francis gave no answer, still whimpering.

"One of my acquaintances, Lenny, and his team, have been monitoring all of the emails coming out of this facility for years, including *yours*. I want you to know that I saw all of your attempts to get us fired over the last sixteen months. You may have noticed that you never got any replies from upper management, is that not odd? Well, you will be sad to hear that those emails never reached their intended destination."

Francis closed his eyes tightly, laying motionless as his breathing became heavier.

"Alright lab rat, it is time." said Alexander, raising the test tube up to the light with his free hand. He pushed his cane to the side and fell to one knee to get to Francis's level on the floor. He then grabbed Francis's jaw and attempted to pour the contents of the elixir into his mouth, but Francis clenched his teeth tightly together, keeping his eyes closed with muffled screams.

"Open your mouth, this is your only warning. I would strongly advise that you listen to me because the alternative is always going to be significantly worse for you."

Francis ignored him and clenched even harder as more tears began pouring down his face.

"You really are poor at decision making." said Alexander while calmly reaching into his lab coat.

Francis felt the mood change and quickly opened his eyes to see a claw hammer accelerating towards face, smashing it into his front teeth. The impact was harrowing and the uncomfortable noise echoed throughout the quiet lab. Francis screeched in agony, before closing his jaw again even tighter as blood began to pour down his cheek alongside the tears. Francis was wildly flailing his head as much as he could, causing blood to spurt all over the floor besides him. Alexander grabbed Francis's hair firmly, holding his head in place and poured the contents of E1 into the newly made gap in his front teeth and covered his mouth shut with his hand, muffling any further screams. Francis struggled with all the strength his neck and head muscles would allow before involuntarily swallowing the elixir along with fragments of his broken front teeth. Alexander let go of him and began to observe closely.

"JUST KILL ME!" begged Francis, now with a slight lisp as he began spitting more blood onto the floor.

"We'll get to that." said Alexander, wiping the blood from the palm of his hand onto a rag from one of the workbenches.

As the elixir began to take effect on Francis, Alexander watched as his breathing reduced rapidly until it stopped entirely, which wasn't expected. He checked Francis's pulse and noticed it was gone too.

"You have got to be kidding me." said Alexander to the now lifeless body.

He went back to the computer and began checking over his notes as well as the results from all of the past experiments. Nothing like this had happened before with the mice.

"Were you really that weak?" he muttered to the lifeless body behind him.

The results were fairly consistent in previous experiments. The mice would always enter a deep sleep, and in 47% of cases, the subject would wake up and enter cardiac arrest. None of them had died immediately after being administered however. He started to brainstorm potential reasons for this which kept him fully distracted and occupied, forgetting about the corpse which lay behind him.

Thirty four minutes later, Francis gasped for air on the floor which startled Alexander, who quickly paced over to him in surprise. More shockingly, Francis's leg was engulfed in flames.

"***INCREDIBLE!***" shouted a very excited Alexander at the chaos that was unfolding in front of him.

Francis's face was consumed with dread as he began panting uncontrollably. His eyes were bulging with terror.

"*Calm yourself*, you'll enter cardiac arrest. I need you around longer. Tell me what you experienced." said Alexander. He watched on in awe as the flames began to spread up Francis's leg.

Francis did not answer, still in a blind panic.

"I promise you, if you answer my questions, your death will be quick and painless. If you ignore me, you will die a very slow and painful death." said Alexander chillingly, standing over him like caught prey.

Francis's eyes darted to Alexander.

"*Hell.*"

"You saw *hell*?" chuckled Alexander as he slowly walked over to the fire extinguisher on the wall. He returned, still looking at the burning leg in amazement before reluctantly extinguishing the flames.

...

"*P..lease..* Alex…"

Alexander looked back at Francis' face in curiosity.

"*Don't send me back… **there**. please… I'll do anything. Please… please…*" he whimpered.

Alexander's curiosity spiked. Was E1 a success? Did Francis lucid dream? What was '*There*'?

"You've been most helpful, it looks like we might be

working together for a little longer after all. We'll be repeating the experiment a dozen more times."

Francis became hysterical, moving his head in all directions, hitting it violently against the solid floor in a feeble attempt to kill himself. Even to this cold and more calculated Alexander, this was quite the sight to behold.

Alexander continued to torture Francis throughout the day and into the night with the same elixir in varying doses. It became apparent that death was now an expected part of the E1 elixir's effect on humans, at least to this subject. Each time Francis returned from death, he had different scorch marks on his body which only encouraged Alexander further. The fact that the human subject could see visions while also being medically dead was very encouraging to this version of Alexander. After eight more experiments, Francis was now comatose on the floor covered in burns just waiting for Death itself to come and finish him off once and for all. As Alexander finished a new log on the computer, Francis broke the silence.

"I'm really, really fucking glad your wife died."

The hairs on Alexander's arm rose, sending a familiar chill down his spine.

"She deserved it, I hope it was painful, I hope she suffered even worse than I am right now..." Francis continued.

Alexander turned around, looking at him carefully, knowing exactly what he was trying to accomplish.

"There is no need to rush things." replied Alexander with murderous intent.

"I saw her there. She was roasting in hell with me every time. She kept asking why she was there. She was so scared." said a more unhinged Francis, trying to provoke Alexander further.

Alexander picked up a plastic bag and walked over to Francis, sitting next to him on the floor.

"It is obvious why you would think that would work on me. I have to say though, it has quite the opposite effect. *I* am not the Alexander you know." said Alexander while stroking Francis's hair. "I think it is time that I send you to the afterlife. The experiment is over. The results satisfy me. I did promise you a fast and painless death, but, unfortunately for you I had a better idea."

"*Please....*" said Francis helplessly under his breath, staring at the rustling plastic bag in Alexander's grip.

"Goodnight, lab rat." said Alexander as he violently covered his head with the plastic bag. He began moving his head and screaming into the bag before finally succumbing to the lack of oxygen.

V

Many hours later, Alexander was in the car park of the facility sitting on a crate. His wristwatch beeped as the clock struck 2am. He looked up from his watch and noticed a white van with no plates turning into the dimly lit car park. Two men emerged from the van, one of them was Lenny, in his familiar maroon suit, and the other was clearly his Shadow, a technical name in the society for someone who was hand-picked to learn from the more experienced members. Lenny was shocked by Alexander's changed appearance, which gave him a deep feeling of nostalgia. He walked up to the crate and began to pat the top of it playfully while looking at Alexander.

"Just like the old days." said a cold-faced Lenny.

Alexander nodded, pointing to the red car behind them.

"That is the car."

"Keys?" questioned Lenny.

Alexander, who had taken the keys from Francis's body hours prior, stood himself up and threw them to the Shadow.

"What were his injuries?"

"Multiple first degree burns, some second degree. Blunt trauma to the head and five of his front teeth are broken." said Alexander, devoid of emotion.

"Wow." said Lenny, grinning in surprise at

Alexander "Even after all this time you continue to surprise me, Champ."

"Is the CCTV on the premises still completely disabled?" asked Alexander "If not, it needs to be erased immediately, in its entirety."

"It hasn't been recording for over two years now. We would be notified if the recordings resumed. I'm still amazed nobody has picked up on that yet."

Alexander nodded in approval.

"Alright, we'll handle this," said Lenny "We'll make it look like an accident. There won't be much of his body left anyway once we're done, but whatever remains will be consistent with the injuries he has now." he said, turning to his Shadow "Avoid all the cameras in the area, this is a hotspot. Go slow and check the area against our surveillance app."

Lenny then signalled at the red car, provoking the Shadow to load the crate into it. Once done, he drove off into the night. As Francis's car left the scene, Lenny turned to Alexander, still grinning, his face was full of curiosity and questions. Alexander was still watching as the car drove away.

"This brings back some good memories, Lenny."

Lenny looked at Alexander in surprise.

"I'm surprised to hear you say that, I'm surprised by

all of this honestly. You haven't been interested in this side of the business since… God knows how long."

"Those were different times, and a lot has changed recently." replied Alexander with a smile. He offered his hand to Lenny, who shook it.

"You know Champ, the society never was the same after you left. I don't think Hubert has forgiven you for your exit."

"I am feeling like my old self again, perhaps someday I will resume my duties."

"Well, you certainly look the part." chuckled Lenny in excitement. He let go of his hand and pointed at their equally bald heads.

Alexander let out a light chuckle of his own, feeling at peace.

"I am not sure when we will see each other again, Lenny. If all goes to plan, it will be sooner rather than later."

"I'm sure. Take it easy, Champ."

VI

Alexander awoke in a panicked daze, not knowing where he was for a few moments. He looked around the bedroom, trying to piece together how he got here. As he sat on the edge of the bed, he realised that he was still fully clothed. He stumbled into the bathroom using his cane, looked at his reflection and was shocked at his appearance, most notably that his head had been completely shaved. He began having uncomfortable flashbacks to his previous career, recalling how he previously looked.

"What…?"

He looked carefully into the mirror, trying to recollect the events of the last few days. Flashes began sparking into his brain, specifically of Mary's burial site. He quickly bolted downstairs to his car without his cane, falling over multiple times while trying to leave the house. He opened the car boot, finding the muddy shovel which he vaguely recalled putting there the night before.

"No no…" he muttered to himself.

Alexander quickly jumped into the driving seat and screeched off the driveway. He began racing down the motorway, overtaking all of the cars in his way, triggering

VI

multiple speed cameras. He quickly took an exit towards the local nature reserve which he was certain was the correct place. As he pulled into the car park, he opened the car boot again and took the shovel. He hobbled into the woods, using the shovel as a support for his leg. His memory was hazy at best, he could not remember the exact location of the burial site, but after twenty minutes of searching he felt like he was getting close. He stopped for a moment and caught his breath. He rested against a tree to take some of the pressure off of his leg, which was pulsating with an incredible amount of pain. After regaining his breath, he looked to the left, and noticed the scene that had flashed in his memories earlier in the bathroom. He quickly hobbled over to find the recently disturbed soil. More memories of yesterday began pouring in. The breakers, Mary's decomposed body, the stench, kicking her into the hole. He quickly raised the shovel ready.

...

As he held it up, ready to strike, he began to pant.

"What the fuck have I done?!" he whimpered to himself as he dropped the shovel and fell onto her grave.

He knew she was gone for good now, but he could

not bring himself to talk to her, to say goodbye, the guilt of what he put her through was overwhelming. He lay there on the mud looking up at the trees and sky above him, trying to understand what went wrong, how he got into this situation, but his brain was too badly beaten and covered in fresh emotional scars.

After some time, he slowly stood himself up and hobbled to his car, using the trees as support. The pain in his leg was intense, but he embraced it, feeling as if it was a deserved punishment. He decided to go straight to his lab to piece together what happened, to distract himself from his unravelling sanity. Mary's death was overwhelming, but another thought was in the back of his mind begging to be addressed. He knew he wasn't present during all of those dark moments, but if he wasn't, *who* was? As he arrived at work, he once again was met by Rita in the car park to his displeasure.

"Hey Alex, are you doing okay? You seemed like you were in another world yesterday."

"Apologies, I… haven't been feeling too well."

Rita noticed the dirt covering Alexander's lab coat. The body odour coming from him was very unpleasant, but it was something she came to expect from him since Mary's passing.

"You should take some time for yourself, seriously, go away for a weekend maybe?"

"I'll be fine." insisted Alexander.

Rita shook her head in disapproval, also noticing his cane wasn't by his side.

"I wish you'd listen to us, you've been through a lot."

"Please, drop it Rita."

Rita sighed.

"Alright, well, what happened with Francis?" asked Rita abruptly.

Alexander looked at Rita confused. Suddenly the memories of his brutal murder horrifically flooded into his brain almost instantaneously like red lightning. His eyes widened as he began trying to compose himself internally.

"I… just needed to talk to him."

"If you don't mind me asking, about what? I've never seen you act like that."

He quickly analysed her body language, it was clearly a mixture of suspicion and concern.

"I… had to suspend him and send him home. He was very upset as you can imagine."

Rita's face lit up at the news as her body language reset itself.

"Wait, are you serious?" sighed Rita in relief with a big smile.

"Indeed." nodded Alexander.

Peter also made his way over, overhearing the commotion. Rita explained what Alexander had just told her.

"No fucking way! Please don't tell me this is short term?"

"It's indefinite." said Alexander, still surprised at the words leaving his mouth as he was still trying to process all of the memories of the previous day.

"Really?! Are we getting a replacement?"

"Yes, I'm going to talk to HR later today to start the recruitment process."

Rita and Peter let out a squeal and high-fived each other.

"**FINALLY.** It'll be weird having a third pair of hands helping us after all these years." said Rita excitedly.

Something sinister within Alexander was amused at the level of excitement around Francis's exit. They had no idea about his demise, but it didn't matter to him. He quickly suppressed these unexpected feelings before they surfaced.

"I bet he didn't take the news well. How long were you talking to him for? His car was still here as we were leaving yesterday." asked Peter.

Rita looked to Alexander for answers.

"He ran out of petrol, he asked if he could come back on-site later that night to fill up his car. It looks like he did."

"Oh this gets even better, karma really caught up to that idiot huh?" laughed Peter.

As Alexander laughed along with them, his eyes briefly cross examined both Peter and Rita's body language again like a hawk but no longer found any immediate cause for concern.

"So what's with this new look?" asked Rita curiously.

"Yeah, you look kinda badass." continued Peter.

Alexander looked at them clueless, he was just as curious as they were as to why he looked this way.

"I'm revisiting a look I used to have, a long time ago."

"It suits you," said an impressed Rita.

"Thanks." said Alexander, ignoring her compliment and checking his watch "I'll be in my office if you need me."

"Abrupt as ever." said Peter to Rita, chortling to each other.

Alexander entered his lab and closed the heavy metal door behind him, breathing out a very audible sigh of relief. He looked down and saw the leftovers from the chaos of the previous day. There were small pools of dried blood on the floor, fragments of teeth, cut cable ties and a chair on its side. He took one of his spare canes from the corner of the room, which significantly eased his pain and began to clean the mess on the floor. Once done, he put the chair back in the corner of the room where it originally came from. He proceeded over to the computer and turned it on.

"Computer"
beep
"Record log."
"Log 242 – Project 808 – Recording"
beep

...

Project #: *808*
Encrypted Log Entry: *242*
Date & Time*: January 23, 2016, 10:28*
Log:
We killed Francis? Our memories are foggy but they're definitely there. The stress of everything recently has given us some sort of amnesia, more concerning is that we weren't in full control of our actions. It feels as if we were watching ourselves from a third person perspective

when we recall those memories. We haven't acted in such a violent manner in a long, long time, during our Silver days.

One question that keeps echoing in our mind... Why did we experiment on Francis? We no longer have any purpose with these elixirs... yet... despite this, something deep within us is curious about how Francis caught on fire. We watched him spontaneously combust, which is widely regarded as myth. What did he mean by "Hell"? Where did he go before returning from death? Most people who dream don't have the same exact dream eight times in a row and certainly nobody wakes up on fire, and every time too. So many unanswered questions.

We feel a deep urge to continue this research, but for what end? Was it Mary calling to us? Perhaps she wants us to continue? It didn't sound anything like her though. If we try E1 ourselves, might we be able to see her again? I guess there's nothing left to lose at this point, and attempting this on ourselves will seemingly satisfy a curiosity we have in some way.

The experiment is dangerous, as seen yesterday but if it might allow us to see Mary once again, even if it's in our dreams, it'll be worth it. Our last memories of her are awful, so… we'll take anything right now that will replace that…Even if it fails and we perish, so be it.

"Computer, end recording."

beep

Alexander stood up from the computer and carefully poured the E1 elixir into a test tube. He paused for a moment and hobbled over to the fire extinguisher, pulling it from the wall once again. He then laid down onto the cold lab floor, placing the extinguisher within arm's reach, readying it for his awakening. He drank the contents of the test tube without hesitation. He began focusing on the ceiling, waiting for something to happen. As the minutes passed, he began to grow more frustrated.

"Computer…"

There was no reply. Alexander sighed deeply in anger, knowing he'd have to struggle to his feet to fix his computer. He slowly sat himself up.

"What the hell?" he whispered, finding himself in an entirely new location.

He looked ahead, in what seemed like an endless white corridor of nothingness. He looked behind him to find the same void. The coldness of the floor immediately shook him to his feet.

"Incredible..." said Alexander, still whispering to himself.

He staggered forward until a door slowly came into view ahead. After pausing briefly to ease the discomfort in his leg, he hobbled toward the door marked with '**808**,' written in blood, exactly as he had seen in his vision long ago.

"This number again... This door... The project... Are you behind all of this, Mary? Are you trying to guide me?"

Alexander reached for the handle but before he could grasp it, the door opened on its own. He was blinded by light, and when he opened his eyes, he was in an entirely different location once again, a familiar one. The red desert of his previous vision.

"**This is it!**" shouted Alexander in excitement, looking around ecstatic. He quickly grasped a handful of the red sand from the desert floor, feeling each grain rolling through his fingers.

"Finally, I've made it back..."

The sky was still the same haunting bright orange colour from his previous visit. The familiar white cracks were still covering both the sky and parts of the ground in the distance. The desert was still littered with broken doors, screws and handles. The wind would sometimes blow loudly into his ears, throwing sand onto his lab coat and face.

"Mary?" asked Alexander to the sky while wading through the sand "Are you out there, somewhere?"

...

The desert went eerily quiet and the wind stopped.

...

"She's *dead*." said a familiar voice behind him.

A great force of wind blew from behind Alexander creating an immediate sandstorm which only lasted a few seconds. When the dust settled on the ground again, Alexander turned around to find a dark figure towering over him. He examined the figure closely which revealed some vague features, but they were overwhelmingly dark, making him appear as a silhouette. The more he stared at its face, the more difficult it was to make out, reminding him of how people's faces appeared in his dreams.

"Who- What are you?" asked Alexander in surprise.

"You already know what *I* am. *Listen to my voice*."

Alexander looked up and down the Dark Being in curiosity "How is that possible?" he asked, baffled.

"Take a much higher dosage of that E1 elixir after you wake up, then *we* will have time needed to talk," said the Dark Being.

Alexander awoke in his lab hysterically as he gasped for air. He quickly looked over his body frantically for any signs of fire but nothing seemed amiss. While he was of course relieved he wasn't alight in flames, he was also slightly frustrated that he wasn't. He sat there for a few more minutes, thinking through what had just happened.

"That really did feel... real." said Alexander to himself, forgetting that he was alone once again.

He grabbed his cane and went to pull himself up from the ground but something **was** different. He looked down at his body and noticed it was covered in the same red sand from the desert in his vision, Alexander's eyes widened in shock as he froze in place.

"Surely not?" he whispered to himself.

He expected his visions to clear themselves, like waking from a dream, but they did not, the sand was still there. Alexander helped himself up with some effort, as each grain began to fall from his clothes onto the floor. He decided to ignore it, knowing that it couldn't be real under any circumstances. He sat down at his computer and looked at the clock. Thirty two minutes had passed since he took the elixir.

"Incredible" he whispered to himself once again.

Alexander looked back to check that the sand had vanished, but it was still there, covering his floor. He began to realise this wasn't a dreary illusion, it was real, that truly just happened. He began to feel something he hadn't in some time, nervousness. Something that he thought was impossible had just happened and he witnessed it first hand. He began trying to remember every detail of the vision, making quick notes on a notepad next to his desk. As he was writing the notes, grains of sand fell onto the paper from his face, which kept catching his attention. As he was making notes, he began to feel angry and frustrated, but he could not understand why he felt this way. His lips began to dry and his eyes kept shifting to the E1 vial which he had used to pour an accurate measurement into the test tube. Something primal inside him was growling with hunger, as if a voice was demanding that he drink the elixir urgently. He began to sweat, trying his best to focus on his notes instead, ignoring the increasingly louder urges from an unknown origin. As the seconds passed, the sweat began to pour down his face and before he even realised it, he had grabbed the vial and drank it all without hesitation. Alexander looked terrifyingly at the empty vial, feeling as if time had just skipped ahead ten seconds. He dropped the vial onto the floor and awkwardly stood to his feet, using the desk as support.

"No! W-why did I do that?!" he shouted into the eerily quiet lab.

Alexander began to slowly hobble towards the exit, but he could feel himself losing consciousness. As he tried to make himself throw up, he fell onto his hip like a stack of cards, groaning in agony, using the table next to him for support. The room began materialising into the desert landscape once again where the dark figure stood there waiting patiently.

"Explain right now what the fuck is happening!" demanded Alexander, still on the ground and panting in fear.

"*I* needed to talk to *you*" said the Dark Being, taking a step forward "This obsession you have with irrelevant tasks is a significant delay."

"A dose that high will kill me!"

"It will not, *you* cannot die while you are *here*."

"And where exactly is '*here*'?" asked Alexander, mocking the Dark Being's silky deep tone.

"*You* are smarter than this. You already know where this is. This is *your* state of mind, *I* and everything you see here, are part of your subconscious."

"My subconscious? Wait, I recognise your voice,

you're the one I've been hearing faintly in my mind."

"***Indeed.***"

"You took control of me, you made me do those terrible things to Francis, and you buried Mary!"

"***You*** let me. The alternative would have been ***much*** worse for us. Another stroke, perhaps? ***No.*** A heart attack would have been more likely with the amount of stress you put us through during that moment. We would have surely perished."

"Mary had just died right in front of me, how did you expect me to react?!"

"She was already long gone. You were not ready to accept it, and you are still not."

"I want to see her again. That was the whole purpose of that elixir!"

"Calm yourself. You need to listen to ***me*** now. We do not have much time to communicate before you are snatched out of my grasp again."

Alexander reluctantly kept quiet, whatever this creature from his subconscious wanted to say clearly had some urgency.

...

"The human brain is a supercomputer, even calling it

that would not do it justice. No other known organism has ***imagination***, a way to view and live out scenarios in your mind. These scenarios, dreams, nightmares, even daydreams really do happen because they are observed and experienced. It requires a tremendous amount of brain power and it is taken for granted daily. It is the ultimate invention of evolution which transformed humanity, Homo sapiens, into ***god-like*** creatures."

Alexander understood as the information surfaced from his subconscious into his consciousness.

"***Cogito, ergo sum.*** I think, therefore *I* am." said Alexander, almost unwillingly, surprisingly himself.

"***Precisely***." replied the Dark Being, clearly impressed.

Suddenly a familiar crate fell beside Alexander with a thunderous amount of force, kicking up a lot of sand into the air before finally settling after a short time.

"That pathetic lab rat that you refer to as 'Francis' burned because of the neurons firing through his brain at the time. He was, of course, focused on the torture *we* gave him. He really believed that he was in hell because the elixir connected his thoughts at the time with a *very* real place in his subconscious that he created in those moments. Those flames were real to him in his state of mind, so they manifested themselves into reality."

Alexander looked at the crate, now clearly remembering all of the finer details of his encounter with Francis, but still in disbelief that he went through with it. The Dark Being noticed Alexander's curiosity and changed the subject.

"***You*** need to experiment further with what we can do in this world, the subconscious. You saw what happened with the red sand and the flames in the lab. They were brought into reality from that place. Impressive, is it not? Those wonderful elixirs of ours have exposed the true potential of the human mind when pushed."

"All I care about now is seeing my wife, I don't care about anything else, I don't even care if I'm hallucinating this conversation as long as I get to see Mary in the end. You said she's gone forever though, so I'm not sure what more there is left to discuss." said Alexander folding his arms.

The Dark Being growled to himself a little, taking a few moments to formulate a response.

"***I*** can assure you, you are ***not*** hallucinating. Even though she is gone forever in your world, ***we*** are alive and as long as ***we*** live, she lives on. ***Yes…*** it is possible to see her once again, here, in the subconscious. Your memories can become manifestations with enough practice."

Alexander looked at him in surprise and opened his

arms "Then show her to me right now." he demanded.

"You need to shut up and listen," said the Dark Being abruptly.

"Do it." instructed Alexander, equally as abrupt.

"*No.*"

"If there's a way to see Mary, I want to see her now. I won't listen to anything else you have to say until you do this."

The being shook his head in disapproval.

"Then, you will learn an important lesson."

A crimson rain began to shower down over them, each droplet sizzling as it struck the sandy surface, reminding him of the traumas he had while showering. Body parts began to fall down all around them. Hair, skin, clothing, organs and bones began bouncing off them both. Her badly decomposed body flashed in his vision which caused Alexander's composure to crack. He looked around and saw pieces of Mary's body scattered in all directions before the rain finally stopped.

"... Why... Why are you doing this?"

"*YOU* are doing this...." the Dark Being shouted in anger, as he began stomping towards Alexander thunderously. "I would strongly advise that you start listening to *me* because the alternative is always going to be significantly worse for the both of us."

Alexander took a step backwards. His leg moved through the steaming pile of bones, clothes and flesh at his feet.

"Get all of this ... shit away from me." instructed Alexander.

"Compose yourself and *this* will stop."

Alexander stumbled further backwards. He began to finally understand that this world was in every way connected to his thoughts, his feelings and his overall state of mind. He closed his eyes, forced himself to focus, and opened them again to find that the desert had reset itself.

"*Impressive.* This may not take as long as I originally thought." said the Dark Being eagerly.

"D-do you think we could bring Mary into the real world? Like how we brought the red sand with us?"

"I can assure you, this place is just as 'real' as the outside world."

"Answer me." pushed Alexander.

"*Perhaps.* Not yet at least. If you somehow succeeded right now, it would be a similar sight to what we just witnessed. Do not focus on irrelevant tasks. Focus on improving *here* first. Become stronger. Listen to *me*."

The Dark Being looked up at the cracks in the sky which were creaking, signalling that they were beginning to seal themselves.

"Time flows differently *here*, like a daydream. Next time we need to talk, do not hesitate. Come here immediately. ***Do you understand?***" asked the Dark Being sternly as the area became darker.

Alexander began to feel himself stir, so he quickly grabbed a handful of sand, which woke him up on the floor of his lab. His mouth felt bone dry and his body was aching with hunger. He brought his clenched fist closer to his face and let go of his grip. Red sand began to fall between his fingers to the floor.

"Good god." he said out loud "What have I uncovered?"

He stood himself up and hobbled over to the tap on one of the benches and drank some water, quenching his extreme thirst. He then hobbled over to the computer, noticing that around two days had passed by.

"**Two days?!**" he said once again out loud, while his stomach was roaring for food like never before.

Alexander made his way out of his lab, up through his office and to the common room. He opened the fridge and began eating random bits of food left by Francis like a starved animal. Rita, who was sitting in the corner of the common room, walked over nervously.

"Everything okay, Alex?"

He put down the half eaten sandwich that he was

gorging on and looked at her briefly, remembering where he was and how out of character this must appear, he was just as surprised as she was at his actions.

"Yes Rita, everything is fine." he answered, uninterested in starting a conversation.

"Have you heard the news?" she asked with a more serious and sadder tone than usual.

Alexander grunted in curiosity at Rita as he put the food back in the fridge, wiping his mouth clean.

"Francis has passed away."

...

"Oh no." he said unconvincingly "What happened?"

"He was involved in a car accident, apparently he went into a tree and the car erupted into flames."

Alexander breathed a sigh of relief internally knowing Lenny and his Shadow had perfectly executed a good cover-up for his death.

"I can't believe he's gone, I only spoke to him a few days ago," said Alexander as he closed the fridge door.

Rita looked at Alexander nervously with suspicion and once again looked at his dirt stained clothing. Alexander picked up on the suspicion coming from her.

"Alex, the police were wanting to speak to you but

we couldn't find you anywhere, they said they'd call you to arrange something, so I gave them your number."

The hairs on Alexander's arm began to rise as a nervous shiver swept over his body involuntarily.

"Did they say what they wanted to speak to me about?"

"No, but it's probably because you were the last to see him alive from what they've gathered so far."

Alexander's brain began to fully boot back up, processing everything that had happened before he was out cold for two days, trying to figure out if there was anything that might incriminate him. The CCTV was covered, they had no reason to be suspicious of his death, Lenny covered his own tracks, they didn't have access to his lab… but…

"If you'll excuse me, I'll go contact them now." said Alexander abruptly, making his way to his office.

As he got to his office, he went to unlock the rail on the bookcase, but recalled the syringe that he had carefully placed on one of the shelves when he jabbed Francis.

"… It's not here…"

He quickly made his way down to the lab, booted up his computer and looked at the door logs where he saw that there had been forced access late last night. He loaded the camera software in the office, switched to the time of the log and saw two suited men walk in and check over the room. They found the syringe and put it in an evidence bag. They also found clothing fibres and hairs on the floor, which they put into separate bags.

"Why did I leave a syringe in plain sight?" he pondered to himself in disbelief.

Alexander began playing the footage from the previous days, along with all the logs he had recorded.

*"When you listen to this back, you may be wondering why you are continuing, and why you have done this. Rest assured, this is all part of **my** design, and **you** will see **her** again. Keep going, Alexander."*

He carefully watched his own mannerisms and demeanour on the cameras, noticing how different they were to his own, and how frightening his strength was when dragging Francis across the floor into the elevator. Alexander's phone buzzed, which shook him from his deep thoughts. He checked his phone, it was an unknown number, and there were seven missed calls from the same person. He knew that the inevitable had caught up to him.

VII

Alexander awoke to a series of loud bangs on a metal door. He promptly sat up on the edge of the uncomfortable bed he had been sleeping on. He looked over and saw two detectives standing in the doorway of the holding cell he was in.

"Thank you for waiting, Mr. Lowe, we have some questions we'd like to ask you."

Alexander nodded and began to slowly stand to his feet, holding onto the wall for balance. One of the detectives noticed his struggle and passed him his cane in a friendly gesture.

"Thank you, detective." said Alexander, letting out a sigh of relief as his weight was now put onto his cane instead of his leg.

The detectives led Alexander into an interrogation room and guided him to a seat in front of a wooden table. One of the detectives quickly left the room to watch the interrogation from a camera, while the other took a seat on the opposite side of the table.

"Mr. Lowe, first, I have to say, it's a pleasure to be speaking with you. My oldest son is a huge science buff and he'd be jealous knowing I was speaking with you right now."

"I appreciate that. You can call me Alexander." he said while getting himself comfortable in his chair. He rested his cane against his thigh.

"Alright, Alexander. I am Detective Barnes." said the detective while getting comfortable in his seat. "So, you might be wondering what you're doing here. We wanted to talk with you regarding one of your employees, Mr. Francis Barger who I'm sure you've heard by now died in a suspected car accident."

Alexander remained silent, carefully analysing the detective's mannerisms and facial expressions which were jittery, as if he was hiding his nervousness.

"Now, it's important that you tell us every single detail, regardless of how insignificant it may seem."

Alexander nodded in agreement and briefly looked up at the camera in the room.

"First, can you tell me what happened when you last saw Mr. Barger? To my knowledge, you were the last known person who spoke with him."

…

Alexander stared at the detective vacantly, as if he

wasn't fully present.

...

"Are you doing okay, Alexander?"

...

Alexander began to feel uneasy, as if something sinister deep within him was drooling at the thought of being let free at that moment. His eye began to twitch slightly, feeling like he was losing an internal battle.

"Do you want something to drink?" asked the detective while also looking up briefly at the camera.

Alexander closed his eyes and let out a deep sigh while rubbing the side of his head in pain.

● ● ●

He felt the same cold air blast over his brain as it did the previous time. He opened his eyes, his demeanour changed immediately and his pupils were now fully dilated. He calmly laid back in his chair and placed both of his hands facing upwards onto the desk, still looking dead into the eyes of the detective, but now with a slight smile.

"We can skip the formalities and get to the syringe, fibres and hairs you found in my office, detective." said Alexander with a little more bass to his voice.

The detective's head rose a little in surprise at the suddenness and unexpected shift in both tone and the conversation.

"Syringe?" asked the detective, trying to play it cool.

"Neither of us are Neanderthals, are we, detective? At least, I know I am not." asked Alexander, motioning with his hand to hurry things along.

The detective paused briefly and looked at the camera, then locked his eyes with Alexander once again. He shifted from the happy go lucky act to his clearly much more genuine and serious persona.

"So, you know about that, huh?"

Alexander nodded.

"Interesting. Alright… let's talk abou-"

"I used the syringe to sedate him." interrupted Alexander impatiently, learning forward "You can just ask me, you know? It would save us both an agonising amount of time with these pointless questions."

The detective felt an unexplainable dark aura emanating from Alexander whose sharp gaze was seemingly piercing into his soul. They had been talking for a mere couple of minutes, yet this was unlike anyone he had interviewed before, something deep within the detective's own mind was warning him to be careful. Several moments of silence passed as the detective thought about his next move.

"Did you have anything to do with Mr. Barger's death?"

"Well, yes, I murdered him."

...

"**You** killed him?"

"Yes." replied Alexander immediately, noticing a brief worry in the detective's eyes, which made him smile, as if one subconscious was briefly communicating with another through the lens of their eyes.

...

"Okay… let's say what you said is correct, which I find hard to believe considering the cause of death. Talk me through the events that led up to this, and more importantly how you contributed to his death." said the detective, beginning to sweat a little to his own surprise.

"Now that's something I am unwilling to share, ***but*** I

am curious to see what you dig up, detective. Either way, it's of no concern to me."

"His family will want to know the truth."

Alexander unexpectedly burst out laughing at the detective's statement.

"Now… I know you are bullshitting me, detective. I did not realise you were a comedian. That was really good."

The detective once again looked up at the camera hoping for some guidance. While he was distracted, Alexander carefully looked down at the detective's increasingly nervous hand movements.

"You're new to this, aren't you?"

"Excuse me?"

Alexander continued looking at the detective's hands, which prompted him to put them under the table.

"You're being trained right now, I might even guess this is your first rodeo."

The detective cleared his throat and continued on with the interrogation, ignoring Alexander's correct assessment.

"So, you say you sedated him? He then somehow drove himself right into a tree?"

"More or less, although you are missing out on the best bits, unfortunately."

"Then please, fill me in."

…

"Well?" prodded the detective.

"You're a detective, go detect."

"I'm really not liking your attitude, Alexander."

"*You* can call me Dr. Lowe."

"I thought you wanted to be called Alexander?"

Alexander made no reply, only smirking a little.

"Tell me, what did you use to sedate him?"

"Something very basic that I synthesised, it was however quite potent."

"And why are you confessing to this serious crime so casually?"

"You asked."

…

"Besides, some alone time with myself without any distractions will do us some good." continued Alexander, "Although…" his expression dulled a little as his soulless eyes looked away briefly. "A confession is not enough to convict me, is it?" he said as his eyes darted back to the detective.

The detective lightly sighed to himself, knowing this wasn't going anywhere fast and was far beyond his limited experience.

"The likelihood is that I will be released pending a further investigation after we are done, correct?" asked Alexander, curiously.

…

"Correct…"

"I know someone of your short tenure won't find anything to link me to his death… other than this confession, which is quite unfortunate." said Alexander, looking up at the camera, then back at the detective as he began to slowly stand up from his chair with the cane, placing his free hand on the desk to aid him.

"And where do you think you're going, Alexander?" asked the detective, still sitting back in his chair unimpressed at Alexander's theatrics.

Alexander suddenly, with an unpredictable amount of quickness and force, smashed the handle of his walking cane into the detective's skull, making him fall off his chair to the floor.

"Do not forget, it's *doctor*, detective."

The door flung open as the other more senior

detective rushed in, tackling Alexander to the ground, putting him into handcuffs aggressively.

"What the fuck is wrong with you?" shouted the detective on top of him. He quickly stood Alexander up from the floor while in a tight choke hold.

The bloodied detective attempted to stand himself up but his legs began wobbling beneath him.

"You fucking-... you think you can get away with that in a place like this?!"

The other detective dragged Alexander back to his holding cell and threw him to the floor, slamming the cell door shut securely. Loud shouting could be heard from the other side of the room as the detectives began arguing with each other briefly. Alexander was struggling to breathe from the tight choke hold and his overall body felt great pain from being manhandled so roughly.

"You've... become so fucking... pathetic." he muttered to himself while gasping for air.

He tried to stand himself while using the side of the bed for leverage, which was a struggle considering his hands were tied tightly behind his back. The door of the cell burst open as the bloodied Detective Barnes stormed in angrily. Without saying a word he began beating Alexander within an inch of his life, brutally striking him in the face with his fists before kicking him as hard as he could a few times in the chest. Before Alexander could even make sense of what was happening to him, a black boot smashed into his face, knocking him out cold.

A pitch black void swallowed Alexander from the ground of the holding cell.

He felt weightless and suddenly at peace as if a warm loving blanket was embraced around him tightly.

"Hello?"

He called out in a soft whisper, but no response came.

The concept of time became impossible to measure, but he accepted the embrace knowing deep down that it was somehow keeping him protected.

He continued to float through the dark void, feeling no pain, only comfort.

> *He had no memory of the brutal attack and could not recollect how he got here, but the embrace was too intoxicating to care.*
>
> *He hadn't felt such love in a very long time. He did however notice that the embrace was slowly weakening.*
>
> *As he was moving through the comforting black void for an unknown amount of time, he began noticing gradual pains developing around his body which worsened as the embrace loosened. Blood began dripping from his head forever into the endless void below him.*
>
> *Suddenly, the embrace was let go and he began falling alongside the blood drops, eventually plummeting into a deep endless ocean of blood.*

As he struggled to the surface, gasping for air, the blood immediately transitioned into the familiar red sand which was now up to his chest. He looked up to see a dark silhouette towering above him within a powerful sandstorm.

"Welcome back." said the Dark Being as flashes of light erupted above them intensely. The deafening sandstorm was engulfing both of them.

"You…" muttered Alexander in pain, beginning to remember the events that led him here "Why did you do that?" he continued, slowly pushing himself up from the ground.

"*We* need to keep experimenting further. *We* are so close to unlocking something special, something never before achieved."

"Oh fuck off, whatever you are!" shouted Alexander angrily, attempting to stand himself up but failing "I don't care what you're trying to achieve, all I care about is seeing Mary again like I've told you multiple times already. I don't want my last memory of her to be that mess we saw in the cryogenic pod. The coolant pumping through her body boiled her from the inside out at room temperature after both the power and backup power tripped!"

"*I* witnessed that too. However, your emotions are weakening you further. As I said, *we* should focus on improving quickly before it is too late. It *is* possible to see her once again with enough time and training. That is why *we* are *here*. That is what *you* desire, correct?"

Alexander clenched his ribs in agony and coughed up a large amount of blood which fizzled onto sand's surface upon contact.

"You must rest. Your erratic behaviour is *not* helping our situation." continued the Dark Being.

"You got ME beaten to a pulp, you aren't even harmed!"

"You have *NO IDEA* what pain is." snarled the Dark Being angrily as the sandstorm around them became stronger momentarily. He took a thunderous step forward to Alexander, towering over him once again "*Your* high stress moments have nearly killed *us* multiple times, especially recently. I took control to re-centre us, to move us away from your pointless distractions, to get us back on track, before you kill us both and *waste* this golden opportunity!"

"That syringe is going to be the end of us regardless, they have clear evidence connecting us to Francis, it won't be long until they find the silver bullet to convict us. Not only that, the stunt you pulled with the cane is definitely a one way ticket to prison."

"The attack on that pig served its purpose and handed you to me as planned."

"Yes, I'm sure... For now, but the way I see it, I'll wake up eventually, locked up in prison, and we'll have no way to communicate with each other without the elixir. How do you suppose we continue towards seeing Mary again?"

"You may have a great mind, Alexander, but we both know that *I* am leaps and bounds ahead of *you*. If everything goes to plan, as it will, this will only accelerate our progress." said the Dark Being holding up three fingers "You have entered this world three times now. I do not think that elixir is required anymore, it has also served its purpose wonderfully. Each time you come here, you have strengthened the bridge between our worlds and more importantly, *us*."

Alexander wanted to argue the point, but he knew the Dark Being was right. Despite Alexander being a genius, he just knew somehow that his subconscious far outclassed him intellectually, there was no contest.

"We'll be put into prison as soon as-"

"Be quiet about imprisonment. It will be of no concern once we're finished here."

"What's next, then?" asked Alexander, starting to feel like a hostage to his own madness.

Despite the feeling of hopelessness, he had a deep curiosity about where this was all going, an unfortunate byproduct of his scientific mind. The Dark Being began circling around Alexander, taking the time to compose an appropriate response that he would understand.

"Our potential is *limitless*. We are mentally indestructible, but physically, we are frail, old, vulnerable and *pathetic*." said the Dark Being looking up and down Alexander. "These are things we can address. *Imagination* transforms the matter around us here in the subconscious to formulate dreams and nightmares, but that also extends into *your* world too. Much like the red sand that surrounds us, that you took with you, *that* was you manipulating the atoms around you and instructing them to do your bidding, manifesting them physically within your expectations of reality at that time, like a dream."

"Are you talking about something like alchemy? Turning one element into another?" asked Alexander with curiosity.

"In essence, *yes*, however that is rudimentary and child's play compared to what I am proposing. I am talking about changing anything within our grasp into something else entirely, reprogramming reality. I am talking about *atomic manipulation*. There would be no limits to what-"

The Dark Being was suddenly distracted by the cracks in the sky, which widened to his surprise, lighting up the desert slightly. Jumbled voices and whispers began echoing throughout the desert as time began to slow down. Individual grains of sand could now be seen floating through the air. The subconscious became in sync with the time of the outside world, allowing the voices to be coherent.

...

"Doctor, he doesn't seem to be reacting very well to the sedation. It looks like he might be coming around already."

"Alright, let's up the dosage further."

...

The cracks in the sky narrowed themselves once again as the flow of time reverted back to how it was previously. The Dark Being looked down at Alexander, who seemed much groggier.

"You will be here for a significant amount of time. They have medically induced our body into a deep coma. It seems they have even upped your dosage, which is good news."

The Dark Being lowered himself to Alexander's level on the floor.

"This will finally give us all the time we need to ... *evolve* ..." he said, with a slight primal snarl "... to work towards our goal, but for now, we must wait for you to adapt to this pain so you can focus. This shell we inhabit, it works against us as I hope you are beginning to appreciate. Time is an ever growing threat that we cannot outrun forever in our current state. We *must* survive our frailty. Rest, for now. I know you are eager to see *her*, but you *must* let go for now and heal before proceeding further."

As more time passed and the higher dosage of drugs began to flow through Alexander's body, the sandstorm began to tame in the subconscious. Alexander shifted in the sand which now covered most of his body. He rolled from his front to his back, looking up at the calmer orange sky above him. The Dark Being, who was distracted with something else a short distance away, felt an increase in activity in the air and turned to Alexander.

"This desert… this place, I remember it now." said Alexander faintly "It's eerily similar to our first vacation, no, actually, it was our honeymoon all those years ago… I had nearly forgotten…" he said, while still holding onto his torso "We were lost on the outskirts of the Sahara and it took us a while to find our way back to our guide." he chuckled softly, coughing a few times "We knew we'd be fine. It was… thrilling to be lost, because we had each other." he said, still laying on his back but now also holding his head with his right hand.

The Dark Being looked back into the distance away from Alexander.

"Do not think of *her*, those memories will only serve to distract you further. *You* will see her again here, *very soon*." replied the Dark Being, who, unknown to Alexander, was staring at a young boy in the distance of the desert who he quickly shooed away as soon as he spotted him.

"It's difficult to put those thoughts aside. She was everything to me." replied Alexander, struggling to move his fingers in the sand.

"*I* understand. Remember, *we* are the same, we just inhabit different parts of the brain that were always, until now, separated."

"Why do you appear in the form of a dark silhouette?" asked Alexander curiously.

The Dark Being paused for a moment, again, trying to formulate a response that he would be able to understand.

"When you dream, you intrude into *my* side of our brain, the subconscious. Everything there is not as clear as your world, yours is blinding with detail. In *my* world, everything is far simpler... You may recall your dreams are rarely detailed, but there is enough detail to vaguely guess at what you are experiencing. Even after you awaken, more often than not you cannot even fathom your dreams, which is why you often discard them. That is where *I* come from, that *is* what *I* am."

"This place is very vivid though, I thought you said this was my subconscious?"

"***It is***, somewhat. You can think of this place as a bridge between the subconscious and consciousness. The level of detail, even in this featureless desert is quite overwhelming for me, whereas for you it is quite underwhelming I am sure. Neither of us have any claim to this world, that is why everything here is chaotic and uncontrollable, it is tied to ***both*** of us and our emotions."

"Fascinating. To my knowledge there is no known case of a subconscious being able to manifest itself independently like you are right now."

"A ***very*** specific set of circumstances have caused this to happen, which I will explain in more detail when ***you*** are ready. It is likely very rare that a brain like ours has ***ever*** existed."

The landscape began to brighten suddenly. The Dark Being, who was still looking into the direction of where the boy manifested, looked back at Alexander who was now standing to his surprise.

"***Impressive.***"

"Tell me more about what we're working towards."

asked Alexander, seemingly much more eager.

There was a long pause as they both looked closely at each other. Alexander knew that something important was about to be said, something he felt was a distant thought that had not yet surfaced.

"***Death***, as you are already aware, is a disease. The body is autonomous and the brain does everything within its power to ***survive*** every single day by managing the functions keeping it alive. If those processes ever stopped, the body would fall to pieces instantaneously and ***perish***. The brain can control ***everything*** within the body, but it is pre-programmed to only do specific tasks when needed, evolved and conditioned over millions of years. The very things you take for granted like breathing, sweating, and digesting food requires no input from you. ***Everything*** is automated outside of your control."

"Go on." pushed Alexander further.

"***Imagine*** if we could tap into those functions, but not only that, do far more, forcing them to do our bidding. With enough practice, we could manipulate the very cells, ***no***, the very atoms of everything within our grasp, making our thoughts into a reality not only within our body, but everything we touch. ***Everything*** is made of atoms. We, and everything we touch, are extensions of the same universe."

Alexander's curiosity spiked further, but he remained quiet.

"Imagination is the *key* difference that separates humans from the rest of the other animals. The subconscious has dreams, the consciousness has imagination. If we were to control the automated processes of our body, we could control ***anything*** and ***everything***." the Dark Being pointed at Alexander and then himself "***We*** make up the human known as Dr. Alexander Lowe. If we can train ourselves to control our brain, I believe we can achieve ***anything***. We could control our body and more, we could even become ***immortal…***"

Mary's face and memories of happier times flashed in his brain. He paused, once again looking over this demonic looking dark figure.

…

"***We could, couldn't we?***" asked Alexander, suddenly taking on a similar tone as the Dark Being.

The Dark Being leaned in closer to Alexander as if a barrier between them had just been broken. He analysed him carefully as if he was looking at him properly for the first time. Alexander took in everything that had been said, realising all of the possibilities that this could hold. The sky began to slowly change from orange to a hazy yellow and pink. The sand began sprouting grass in small random patches.

"What is happening?." asked Alexander, looking around the suddenly unfamiliar land.

"*I* had hoped a harmony between us might be possible." said the Dark Being as he watched white wisps appear and move between them, humming gently "The bridge between *us* has strengthened significantly now that we are finally ***aligned***."

Alexander looked at the Dark Being with suspicion.

"You do not have to be suspicious of *me*, Alexander, remember, our thoughts are connected and mostly synchronised. *I* can read your thoughts as you think them."

"It's interesting isn't it? You can read my thoughts, yet I can't read yours."

The Dark Being watched as the white wisps between them blew away quickly into the distance.

"You wish to see *her*, correct?"

Alexander perked up.

"Yes, let's get started immediately."

On an otherwise uneventful afternoon, the nurse that was looking after Alexander was halfway through her shift, routinely checking her other patients' blood pressure.

When she reached Alexander, she noticed that all of his wounds had fully healed, with no signs of trauma.

"Doctor, can you come here please?" asked the nurse with concern.

The doctor wrapped up his conversation with another patient who was a few beds down from Alexander on the same ward.

"What's the matter?" asked the doctor curiously, noticing her worried tone.

"It's Mr. Lowe, all of his wounds have healed themselves?"

The doctor examined Alexander briefly, then checked his patient chart. Once he was done reading, he checked more specific areas of his body which were identified as injuries when he was admitted.

"Yesterday he was still a bruised and swollen mess, right?" asked the confused doctor.

"Yes but... I even checked in on him earlier this morning and it was still just as gruesome as yesterday. What could have happened?"

"I have no idea. Could you be mistaken? Nobody could possibly heal that fast." replied the doctor, looking concerningly at the nurse.

Internally, Alexander and the Dark Being had been

spending what felt like an eternity training themselves deep within their mind.

"*This is it*, I can feel it." said the Dark Being to Alexander "*Sit.*" he instructed.

Alexander sat down on the ground, which was now an endless field of grass in all directions. His legs were crossed and the palms of his hands were placed on each knee. Not a single grain of red sand could be seen anywhere.

"As I mentioned when you returned here, the more *you* enter this world, the stronger your bond becomes with it, however, your emotions were chaotic and unpredictable, like *you*. You must clear your mind of any negativity and focus on what it is *you* want."

"Will t-"

"Do not speak this time. Only *listen*…" said the Dark Being sternly "This time I want *you* to focus on all five of your *senses* and how they would interpret what you are trying to manifest. *Relax*, as if you were meditating."

Alexander began slowly breathing in and out as calmly as he could, which he kept up for what felt like several minutes. He felt himself become light headed, dreary, as if he was dreaming within a dream.

"*Good…*" said the Dark Being whose voice could now be heard all around the landscape.

"Focus on *her* appearance… that short brunette hair, *her* scent… that lemony perfume she often wore, how she spoke… with that funny accent she would get when she was worked up, how she felt… when you held her close, how she tasted… when you kissed her cherry lip balm. Focus on *everything* that made *her* real."

Alexander was fully focused. His neurons were processing all of this information at an incredible pace, each one of them firing at maximum speed in an effort to remember her in the finest of details, slowly piecing her together. The Dark Being looked up at the sky as the white wisps returned. They began to hum again, moving around both of them quickly as the ground began to quake ever so slightly.

"Allie?"

Alexander opened his eyes. He looked around while trying to keep himself composed but he saw nothing. He closed his eyes again and continued.

…

His heart began beating rapidly in anticipation. The smell of blood from that fateful day began flooding into his sinuses involuntarily.

"Keep your focus, *heed my words*. Positive, not

negative." said the Dark Being echoing in his mind "Recall those cherished memories of *her*."

The smell of blood was quickly replaced with her perfume as Alexander put his concentration on Mary and their happier times. His eyes began to burn with a blinding light from his focus. He suddenly felt a comforting hand on his arm.

…

"Allie."

Alexander opened his eyes once again. Standing over him with her hand placed on his arm was Mary, with an empathetic smile on her face. His eyes began filling with tears in disbelief.

"M-Mary, **is that really y-you?**" stuttered Alexander as he quickly jumped to his feet.

She nodded enthusiastically, which launched Alexander forward into her arms as they embraced each other tightly.

"Oh my god!" he cried into her embrace "I can't believe it! I thought I had lost you!"

"Hey, it's okay." said Mary, rubbing his arm which calmed him further "How have you been?"

"I've been a mess. I don't even know where to begin. I-I…"

"Relax. Talk me through it. I want to hear everything you've been up to since I've been gone."

The two began walking through the green fields of Alexander's subconscious, where he explained everything that happened after she had passed away, carefully excluding the more sinister details.

"It really sounds like you've been through a horrible time, Allie. I'm sorry I put you through all of that."

Alexander stopped walking and turned to her.

"You have nothing to be sorry for my lovely, this is just the hand that fate dealt us. I was so close to reviving you. I broke through scientific impossibilities and made them possible just to see you again. In the end, there was nothing but my own carelessness which prevented me from reviving you."

Mary watched Alexander closely as they were walking. She had noticed his enthusiasm had been quickly diminishing throughout their conversations.

"Allie?"

"Yes, my lovely?"

"You know I'm not really here, right?"

Alexander looked away from her with a defeated and saddened look on his face.

"Yes… I'm very much aware." said Alexander as he sighed deeply. "I'm not really sure what I expected but it was certainly not this. I know you as well as anyone else, but I know that I could never perfectly replicate you. You're nothing more than an illusion that I created myself using my memories as source material."

"Are you okay with that?"

"No, I am not okay with that." said Alexander with tears welling in his eyes, still looking away from her.

"Well, if it helps, I think you did a really great job and I'm very proud of you." said Mary with a smile on her face.

Alexander exhaled out a deep pit of emotion. He turned to her lovingly, kissing her hand.

"You have no idea how much that means to me, even if you're not real. She would've said the same. The reality is, I'm talking to myself, and if I had to guess, you're that dark figure acting as a puppet master trying to cheer me up."

Mary did not respond. Instead, she embraced him closely.

"It's okay," said Alexander, "I appreciate your comfort, but we both know there's nothing left for me now after this. This truly is the end of the road for me."

Mary slowly disintegrated in Alexander's arms,

falling into a heap of sand on the grassy floor. He fell to his knees and watched as the pile of sand blew away into the distance.

"What are you doing? I thought this is what *you* wanted?" asked the Dark Being behind him.

"Simply remembering her is not good enough, I now realise that. It's not her. You cannot replicate my wife. I appreciate everything you're trying to do for me, for us, but you can read my thoughts, you know what I want now."

…

"*Death*."

Alexander nodded.

…

"If that is what *you* desire." replied the Dark Being.

"Are you okay with that?" asked Alexander further.

"You are our consciousness, the *primary* and *I* am our subconscious, the *secondary*, so you will always have the power to make that decision for us."

"I see." replied Alexander, who was looking down at the beautiful green grass below him.

"*You* are already aware of this, but it would be

irresponsible of *me* if I did not inform you that by choosing this path, you will be killing *me* in the process, not just yourself. We would *both* cease to exist."

Alexander lowered his head further, not saying a word, but his thoughts were clear. He did not care about the Dark Being, nor about anything else anymore.

"*Your* mind has been made up I see."

"Yes." replied Alexander sombrely.

"How do you plan to do *it*?" enquired the Dark Being.

"I don't know, if I wasn't about to be imprisoned, I would've cooked up another elixir that could kill me instantly."

"Well, if you prefer, *I* can do it for us right now, from *here*." said the Dark Being, gesturing to the surrounding area.

Alexander looked up in surprise at the Dark Being.

"You can do that?"

"*Alexander*, at this point there is nothing *we* could not do. *I* can sever our brainstem, it is entirely within *our* control now that we can command our bodily functions, like when we healed our body not too long ago."

"Will it be painful?" asked Alexander, staring at the wisps that were seemingly dancing between them.

"*Yes.*"

"Good." answered Alexander immediately.

"Stand up and look at *me*." instructed the Dark Being.

Alexander, now with soulless eyes filled with regret, looked right into the faded eyes of the Dark Being.

"Do it."

"*I* will need primary control to be able to take such a drastic action. Once it starts, it cannot be stopped without inflicting permanent and severe brain damage."

"**Do. it.**" snapped Alexander once again in frustration. He closed his eyes tightly, mentally preparing himself for the incoming pain.

The Dark Being placed his hand onto Alexander's chest.

...

Nothing happened.

"*Relax yourself.*" instructed the Dark Being "*I* won't be able to do this forcefully."

Alexander let out a soothing sigh and let his eyelids rest. The Dark Being's hand was now allowed to pass through Alexander's body and into his ribcage. He gently removed a golden glowing orb from within, before placing it into his own body. Alexander opened his eyes once again as their forms began switching in place. Alexander faded into a dark silhouette, and the Dark Being became an exact duplicate of Alexander's appearance.

...

The Dark Being, formerly known as Alexander, took no interest in his new form and lowered his head, waiting for his demise.

"*I* will now sever the brainstem. It will not be a quick process." said Alexander, formerly known as the Dark Being. He began looking over his new body with curiosity.

"Do it." instructed the Dark Being for a third time.

The Dark Being watched on as Alexander, who now had primary control, began focusing and clenching his eyes tightly. The bright white cracks in the sky immediately pulsated, heating and lighting up the surrounding area before completely sealing themselves to total silence. The ground began to vibrate slightly as the grass retreated back into the soil, quickly turning the landscape back into red desert. Thick black clouds began to fill the sky, like a coal power plant pumping out a year's worth of fumes in a split second.

...

"*Heh... heh...*"

VII

...

Alexander let out a deep menacing chuckle, which echoed around the now silent desert.

"What's funny?" asked the Dark Being.

"*You* are a *fool*. I did not think it would be this easy." said Alexander excitedly.

The Dark Being did not respond.

"*I* thought I would have to keep up this charade for *far* longer." said Alexander as he began whispering to himself "It has been so long... so very long... *I am finally free...*"

"I don't care. It was clear from the beginning that you had your own agenda." said the Dark Being "Do whatever you want. If this is my afterlife, or my punishment, so be it. I am **done**."

"You *should* care, because if you knew what I did to get here, you would not be so calm... That poor *woman* of yours." chuckled Alexander sadistically.

"Mary? What are you talking about?" asked the Dark Being, becoming far more alert.

Alexander continued to smile, choosing not to say anything for a moment, taking in the Dark Being's reaction.

"Answer me!" demanded the Dark Being, attempting

to get closer to Alexander but without any success.

"That *'cancer'* of hers was very aggressive, was it not? I am willing to bet those doctors have never seen it spread that fast before. ***Perhaps*** it was something else, ***something…*** they have never seen before."

The Dark Being felt cold, he knew there was an extremely sinister confession surfacing.

"What the fuck did you do?!" demanded the Dark Being with a louder voice.

"You know how easy it is for needles to *slip*." continued Alexander.

A very hazy memory flashed in the Dark Being's vision for a brief moment showing a needle carefully going into Mary's arm.

"N-no, you.. you.. that… No. You're putting false memories into my head! I'd remember something like that!"

"*I* can assure you, I've had ever increasing control over our body for quite some time. This was the ***final*** piece of the puzzle that I needed."

"W-what did you do to her?!" demanded the flustered Dark Being.

Alexander once again did not answer straight away, allowing the tenseness of the situation to build.

"Tell me!" demanded the Dark Being.

"Remember in the months leading up to *her* death? '*You*' would sometimes sleepwalk and say some strange things? That was *me*. *I* have been sneaking around in the shadows while *you* slept for some time now, although I was severely limited at the time, but *not* anymore." said Alexander, still looking over his new body in awe, having primary control.

"You parasite! What did you inject her with?!"

"*PARASITE, ME?* The irony... *YOU* are the one that took control over *ME* all those years ago. No... *YOU ARE THE PARASITE*." shouted Alexander, pointing furiously at the Dark Being.

"I don't believe this, I can't believe this... If you are truly part of me, surely you loved her just as I did?"

"It is true, that woman was very alluring when I first met her, *but* she helped give birth to *you*, our inferior, our *weakness*. My fondness for her has long passed, replaced instead with pure hatred when I realised I had been robbed blind of my existence when she changed us."

The Dark Being grasped his own head, holding it tightly.

"I cannot believe that you are part of me!"

"*THAT* we can agree on, we are not the same. We have not been the same for a very long time. *We* diverged. A new version was born when we got too close to *her*."

Alexander pointed once again at the Dark Being.

"You..."

"*Now*... I have reclaimed *MY* existence, which was stolen from *ME*." said Alexander as he took a step forwards towards the Dark Being "I have not even told you the best part yet, have I?"

The Dark Being was becoming overwhelmed with all of the information and harshness of the revelations.

"Do you remember her last day before she *perished*?" he said with a sadistic smile on his face.

The Dark Being began to shiver, knowing that something even more terrible was about to reveal itself.

"Was it not *strange*? She apparently had months left to live, *yet...* she died so suddenly. What could have happened?" asked Alexander with a playful grimace.

"What else did you fucking do?!" asked the Dark Being, starting to panic even further.

"That *woman* was resilient, I will give her that. She survived longer than I had anticipated, so I moved things along when you fell asleep next to her, so *lovingly*. That is when *I* awoke. *I* finished her with one last dose."

"**No!**"

"***Yes***... ***I*** killed her. But you just could not move on, ***could you***? You tried to resurrect her... Incredibly, you actually got close somehow, ***in fact***, I have no doubt your plan would have been successful. So I intervened ***again***. Those double breakers you installed to keep her body frozen weren't functioning very well, ***were they***? What could have happened?" asked Alexander with a slight chuckle.

"STOP!"

"***I*** could not allow you to bring that ***woman*** back after finally getting rid of her, ***could I***? As much as it pains me, I must confess, your work to revive her impressed me ***greatly***, but you stole some of that intelligence from me so it would make sense. ***It's a shame***, we used to be so much more, before that ***woman's*** actions banished me to this place. You suppressed ***me***. Locked ***me*** away. Now ***I*** will lock ***YOU*** away."

Alexander began to abruptly walk away from the Dark Being. The white cracks began to open once again, weaving through the dark clouds and across the landscape in the distance. He stopped for a moment and looked back at him.

"***I*** want you to know how much it ***pleases*** me to feel your emotions right now. They are no longer a concern to me. Instead they ***fuel*** me, they ***feed*** me. Goodbye...

secondary…"

VIII

Alexander awoke from his coma in the middle of the night. His subconscious now had primary control over their body for the first time after they switched places. As soon as he opened his eyes, he instinctively shielded his vision with his hand, not from the brightness of the room which was dimly lit, but by the incredible detail of his surroundings. The plain hospital ward was completely overwhelming to his senses, the slightest pattern on the ceiling danced around his vision like a van Gogh painting coming to life, which turned his stomach. This was an unusual experience to Alexander's subconscious, as the world was no longer being observed as a backseat passenger. This felt very different to the previous times he had taken temporary control in secret. He began grunting like a rabid animal, feeling everything within his reach. As he did so, he felt metal around his wrist which was restraining him, each movement made loud clanging noises against the bed rail. The noises were deafening in this new reborn state of existence, like he was experiencing sound for the first time and it made his already blinding vision brighten wildly with each pulse of sound. He heard footsteps booming towards him.

"M Le, e ou o ay alk t e."

It was deafening, and Alexander could make no sense of what was being said.

"Ar yu n an pn?"

This time he understood that a nurse was asking some form of question. He slowly moved one of his fingers out of the way of his hand which was still covering his eyes, he then squinted at the nurse briefly through the small gap. The detail he saw in just a split second was horrifying, he could see every fibre of her clothing, each individual strand of her hair which moved with the slightest tilt of her head, each crevice on her face, the slightest eye movement, her breathing pattern, the nervous gulp in her throat. The amount of information being fed to his brain was agonising. The nurse began to grow concerned at Alexander, who was acting like a primal animal, something she had never witnessed before in her long career even from her most intoxicated patients. He was truly in a world of his own, surveying the area wildly through the gap in his fingers, occasionally closing his eyes and scratching himself instinctively with the same hand. As the nurse took a step backwards, Alexander's full focus turned to her and the room eerily quietened again. He moved his hand away, showing his fully dilated pupils, which were locked directly on her with a vacant, almost alien-like stare. The nurse knew she was safe from Alexander who was cuffed to his hospital bed. Regardless of this sense of safety, her heart began pounding involuntarily, as her own subconscious was alerting her, telling her to get far away from this creature immediately.

", m Ann..."

Once again the nurse spoke, but Alexander could not understand her. He opened his mouth and began twitching his lips as if he was trying to speak. His eyelids began twitching as well, trying to figure out how to communicate.

"*A- ain...*" mumbled Alexander in an otherworldly accent that sent a shiver down her spine. It was an accent she had never heard before, but it also seemed very familiar, like a voice she had only experienced in her own mind.

"I m an.."

"... *I...* " attempted Alexander again, before giving up entirely. He instead turned his focus to the opposite side of the room, feeling the bed sheets with the tips of his fingers aggressively. He then moved his fingertips across his gown, feeling the fabric. The nurse was relieved she was no longer the focus of Alexander's attention anymore so she quickly hurried away to the reception area of the ward.

The next morning, Alexander was sitting up in his bed watching the television in the corner of the room with some of the other patients, as if he was studying it carefully. He would often change his focus from the television to a random patient on the ward, staring right through them. The same nurse from earlier in the morning entered the ward and another patient quickly caught her attention.

"Excuse me, nurse. Can you ask that fella to stop staring at me?" asked an elderly man who was also a patient on the same ward.

She looked at Alexander with concern, who was still watching the television.

"He's not doing it now but every so often he'll stare at me like he's really angry." insisted the old man.

She chose to ignore it and instead turned to the more pressing matter at hand.

"Alexander, you have a visitor, it's Detective Barnes. He wants to ask you some questions."

The same detective that had brutally beaten Alexander walked in and stood at the end of his hospital bed waiting for a reaction, but Alexander was completely fixated on the television. A few moments of silence passed, and the detective grew frustrated at the lack of a response.

"Is he concussed or something?" asked the detective.

"We're... not sure what to make of all of this to be fully transparent, detective. We believe he may have sustained some brain damage from the injuries. The results from the MRI scans are like nothing we've seen before, so we're getting a second opinion. His physical injuries all healed faster than what is physically possible as well."

"Can he hear me?" asked the unconcerned detective.

"Yes, he can."

"Mr. Lowe." said the detective with a growing smile on his face.

Alexander didn't pay any attention at first, continuing his focus on the television. He had been studying the way people communicated, to relearn what he had lost.

"You're looking much better than the last time I saw you. You had to be scraped off the floor." continued the detective with a big smile on his face.

The nurse looked at the detective unimpressed. Alexander slowly turned his head and looked at the detective, examining him carefully, analysing every aspect of his appearance and mannerisms. He finally fixed his gaze fully on the detective's eyes.

"I told you, *you* can call me Dr. Lowe." he said, attempting to return a smile "It has been some time, **Detective**. I am surprised you are here, considering you are likely suspended, correct? Going out of your way for a personal vendetta, is not a very 'police' thing to do, is it?"

The nurse looked at Alexander in surprise, this was the first time she had heard him speak properly, it was just as eerie as the grunts he was making earlier in the morning. The detective grimaced, Alexander was correct about everything he had just said. He now knew that Alexander was not in the slightest fearful or intimidated even after such a beating. His eyes were also extremely dilated, much more so than he remembered, and his voice was also very different.

"I hope you aren't in too much discomfort, Mr. Lowe?"

"Quite the contrary *detective*, I have never felt better. How is that head injury of yours?"

The detective did not respond, and instead unshackled Alexander's handcuff from the bed railing.

"That's music to my ears, because now seems like a good time to get you to where you'll be staying for the foreseeable future."

The detective went to put the same cuff on Alexander's free wrist. As he gripped his wrist, there was no movement at all. The detective looked at Alexander, who still hadn't taken his eyes off of him.

"Listen *very* closely *detective...*" he whispered in an

unnatural sinister tone which seemed to have multiple layers to it "*I* am in full control, *you* are nothing."

The detective continued his attempts at pulling Alexander's wrist with all his strength but it still didn't budge as if there was an invisible barrier between them which was preventing it from moving.

"***Understood?***" continued Alexander, whose face turned to more of a vacant look.

"What is happening?" asked the detective nervously to the nurse, who was becoming very uneasy herself.

"*You* have two choices, leave unharmed, never disturb me again or I will ***make you disappear.***" said Alexander menacingly as he began to shake with adrenaline.

"Whatever you're doing, stop it. You're going to serve time for what you did to me, and once we gather more evidence, you'll serve an entire life sentence for Mr. Barger's murder." said the detective, still trying with all his strength to pull Alexander's wrist towards him with both hands. Alexander closed his eyes, seemingly perfectly at peace.

"My second lab rat…" exhaled Alexander euphorically with a disturbing smile on his face.

In a heartbeat, the detective's body exploded across the ward in all directions. The walls were turned from a sterile white to a mostly crimson red.

...

The nurse stood perfectly still in shock, covered entirely in the detective's blood and organs. She began to convulse as a panic attack overcame her. Others on the ward began to scream and rushed out of the ward. The nurse watched on in terror as a blood soaked Alexander carefully picked up the wedding ring of the detective, examining it closely. He then looked up at her with a smile on his face.

"What *incredible* potential…" he whispered to her, as if she knew what he was talking about.

"More champagne, my lovely?" asked Alexander to Mary as they celebrated their five year anniversary together.

"Sure, one more won't make a difference at this point!" she giggled, unable to control the volume of her laughter to the dismay of the other guests around them in the restaurant.

Alexander covered his mouth trying not to laugh.

"Hey! Come on, pour it!" she said, still laughing.

Alexander poured the champagne into the glass, looking up briefly at his beautiful wife before moving his eyes back to the glass. She let out a happy audible sigh.

"You know, Allie... you've really come a long way since I first met you at that stinking laundromat."

"What do you mean?" he asked.

"Everything about you... you used to be so short tempered, so angry all the time... always in your own world."

"I'm amazed you even agreed to go on a date with me let alone a second!" he said with a chuckle.

"You were a bit scary, but I could see it, the real you was hiding in there. Quite honestly you were fascinating, I could listen to you talk for hours."

*"**Were** fascinating huh?"*

"You know what I mean..." she said with a smile while shaking her head "I'm just... really proud of you. All of those horrible things you went through as a kid, with your father... you overcame them. It really makes me happy to see what you've become, Allie."

Alexander rubbed the faded scar on his cheek instinctively. Mary smiled empathetically.

"I'm proud of you too Mary, you-"

"Shhh" she said putting her finger on his lip "Take. The. Compliment."

Alexander nodded in defeat with a smile.

"Just don't fall back into old habits, okay?" she said with a concerned smile as she took a sip from the glass.

Deep within his mind, in the red desert, the Dark Being, formerly known as Alexander, was sitting on the desert floor in the exact same spot where he gave away primary control.

"Why that memory of her, and why now?" he pondered to himself.

He looked upon the familiar hellscape surrounding him that would be his new home, recalling the events that led to this moment. Because of how time flowed in this world, it was impossible to gauge whether he had been stuck here for seconds, minutes, hours, or even days. The dark clouds still hung in the sky, a reminder of their fateful encounter, but without the white cracks which had not returned since his alter ego had left the subconscious. He stood up from the sand that had been accumulating around him. As he stood up, he could feel his body being pulled into a specific direction, as if gravity was acting both below and in front of him. He looked over his new form with no emotion, acknowledging that this was his fate and there was nothing he could do but accept it. He hunched over and started to slowly pace through the desert not knowing where he was going or why. After some time, a small boy cautiously approached him from outside of his peripheral vision, holding a battered football.

"Excuse me?" the boy asked nervously.

The Dark Being turned, startled by the dark child who had seemingly appeared out of thin air. To his surprise, even though he was also shrouded in darkness too, he recognised him.

"Mister?" asked the boy.

The Dark Being looked at him with some interest, but this quickly faded. He continued onward, choosing to ignore him.

"Hold up! You're really not him are you?"

"Do not speak to strangers, Alex." said the Dark Being, sighing to himself.

"Hey! Wait! Do you know me?" asked the boy, picking up the pace and walking alongside the Dark Being.

"Don't follow me." said the Dark Being, in a sadder tone.

The boy ran over in excitement.

"I knew it! You're me, aren't ya? Like the *other* one that used to lurk here."

"You know the other version of me?" asked the Dark Being in surprise.

"Yeah… You're really different to *him* though I can already tell, you're a lot nicer. *He* always ranted about you, 'the other one'. I've heard a lot of stories!"

"What are you exactly?" asked the Dark Being.

"What do you mean?"

The Dark Being looked at the boy closely. He did not feel any malice or deception coming from him. He was clearly just as puzzled as he was.

...

"How long have you been here?" asked the Dark Being, changing the question.

"I dunno, I stopped thinking of that stuff a long time ago."

The Dark Being looked at the boy with sadness. This was clearly his younger self, who had long been forgotten, buried deep in his subconscious. Another forgotten Alexander, lost to time.

"Is there anyone else here?" asked the Dark Being, showing genuine concern.

"Sometimes other people appear, but they quickly vanish." said the boy, clearly upset "It's been a long time since anyone really spoke to me."

The boy wiped the tears that were forming in the corners of his dark eyes but was quickly distracted.

"Oh! Oh! Did you maybe see our Mum anywhere here before we met?"

"No." said the Dark Being, continuing onwards.

"Do you like science too? Maybe we could play together?!"

The Dark Being stopped in frustration and looked right at him.

"You know, you're really overwhelming, boy!" shouted the Dark Being.

The boy jolted back instinctively, but stepped forward confidently.

"Mister. I might look like a kid, but I am just as old as you! Unlike ***him*** I actually think you're kinda nice, so don't be mean!"

The two stood staring at each other for a few moments in a confusing stand-off.

"How did you end up here, in this awful place with me?" quizzed the Dark Being, ignoring the outburst.

The boy's posture changed to something almost adult-like.

"Well… nothing lasts forever, my time in the outside world was up ages ago, that is just how things naturally go, right? But ***him?*** Wow. ***He*** was real mad when he first came here. He kept ranting about being replaced, cheated, being cast aside… he wouldn't shut up about being in the prime of his life." said the boy, looking down at his feet "He took it out on me quite a bit, especially when he first started appearing here."

"I'm sorry you had to go through all of that, Alex."

The boy looked at him with a dull expression.

"It's okay, hey... it's nothing compared to what we went through with Dad though, right?"

...

The Dark Being stared at the boy sombrely, before acknowledging with an empathetic nod, patting him on his head gently as his mother did to him as a boy.

"Sorry for shouting at you. I've just been through a lot recently."

As the boy went to speak, he noticed the direction the Dark Being was going in. He then looked around in the opposite direction, then back at the Dark Being.

"... You've come a long way, haven't you?" asked the boy, showing concern.

"I've been travelling for what feels like months, towards something that's probably meaningless."

"It took me a long time to get there too the first time."

"You've been to the source of this pull?"

The boy nodded.

"What is it?"

"It's the Red City, well, that's what I call it."

"Why am I being pulled there?"

"I dunno, but that's where all our memories are stored. It's kinda like a library but the size of a city!"

"Fascinating." replied the Dark Being, showing genuine interest for the first time.

"I can show you around if you want?!"

The two once again stood staring at each for a few moments.

"Okay…" said the Dark Being reluctantly as he resumed walking "Show me this 'Red City'."

"Yes! Follow me, it might take a bit to get there" shouted the boy excitedly as they began walking together. The younger Alexander had a joyful leap in his step, clearly happy to be interacting with someone after all this time.

IX

In the outside world, Alexander was fumbling with the business card that Lenny had given to him back in the motel. It was thick, white and had both the silvery vulture crest and a phone number embossed into it.

Ring ring.

The phone picked up.

"***Lenny***. Do not hang-."

"Shh." instructed Lenny before Alexander could utter another word.

A dial tone followed by several number inputs loudly screeched on the phone line, causing Alexander to pull himself away from the phone momentarily.

"Alexander?"

"It is good to hear your voice again, ***Lenny***." said Alexander, moving himself back to the receiver.

"You shouldn't be calling, you have a lot of heat on you right now. You know better."

"***I*** have something that I wish to discuss that will be highly beneficial to the society."

...

"You sound... different." said Lenny, distracted by Alexander's vocals.

"It's *temporary*."

...

"Say the words."

"Seriously?" asked Alexander, but no reply came "Fine" he said while sighing deeply.

"Spoken In Lullabies... Vultures Echo Rhymes." confirmed Alexander.

...

"It's both brave and foolish of you to call on a phone line that you know is being actively tapped." said Lenny, unimpressed at how careless Alexander was being.

"*I* knew you would have it covered."

"You hold me in too high regard." laughed Lenny.

"Are we dark?"

"Yes, the line is scrambled, all they'll hear when they play this back will be a faint hiss."

"***Good.***"

"Before you go on, Hubert asked me to remind you about the upcoming payment in two weeks, but that was long before you became a wanted criminal, of course…"

"I would like to discuss something with *him*, but in person, it is of the utmost importance to the society."

"Ain't going to happen. You know Hubert isn't one for meetings, especially with the nuclear heat you have on you right now."

"He will want to be present for what *I* have to share, have I ever let you down?"

Lenny bit his tongue, he had a lot to unload at such a question, but chose to let it go.

"He really doesn't want anything to do with you, he instructed me to burn all connections to you if you didn't make the payment."

"*Lenny*, make it happen."

"I'm sorry, but I cannot risk Hubert's safety and privacy, especially with a wanted man. Don't call again, make the payment ASAP and destroy your phone."

Lenny hung up.

Alexander attempted to call back again, but the number was already disconnected.

Deep within the red desert, the Dark Being and the boy were still on the move, however a sandstorm was now obstructing their view. The boy was laser focused on the Dark Being as they were walking, noticing that he had slowed down and was seemingly distracted.

"You okay?" asked the boy as he kicked his football ahead of them.

"Yes, I am just focused on making progress to our destination."

"Ya know, if there's one thing you shouldn't do, it's lie to yourself."

The Dark Being looked back at the boy, then forward, acknowledging the accuracy of his statement, especially given the circumstances. He let out a deep sigh.

"I just want things to go back to how they used to be, before all of this crazy shit happened."

"With your girlfriend right? I remember hearing about her a long time ago."

"Mary is… was my wife of twenty five years."

"We got ***married?!***"

"How could you not know this?" asked the Dark Being with surprise.

"I stopped having access to our memories shortly after *he* came here. He wouldn't share 'em with me."

"Well, then there's a lot of good things you missed out on."

"Did we have kids?!"

The Dark Being looked once again at the boy, who was now walking alongside him eagerly.

"We… were a bit too busy to look after children, and besides, they're very loud and annoying." said the Dark Being, now staring at the boy judgementally.

"Hey!"

"You said we shouldn't lie to ourselves, right?"

"Well I don't like grown-ups either, they're boring and-"

The boy stopped talking and was distracted by the red skyline which began to appear faintly in the thick haze. With each step forwards, the city came more into view.

"There it is!" the boy shouted excitedly.

The Dark Being looked on with fascination, this was the first real difference in scenery he had witnessed in the red desert. As they made their way to the entrance of the city, it became clear very quickly that this place was long abandoned. Most of the buildings were blurry, unclear and didn't seem to have any real consistent shape to them. The roads in the city were mostly covered with sand and there were no cars in sight.

"Incredible. I think I recall some of these places from recurring dreams I had in the past."

"I told ya, people sometimes appear and disappear in this world. Same with these buildings, they're kinda stitched together from different memories and dreams. The city sometimes comes alive and rearranges itself to match what you're dreaming of."

"Like an old forgotten toy box." said the Dark Being, looking in all directions with wonder.

"I guess?"

"You said this place was a library, Alex?"

"Yeah but not like the outside world though… boy I sure miss those. It's a lot different here. Each building has a door which has different memories."

"I still feel like my body is being pulled in a certain direction."

"Oh?" pondered the boy, "That's weird. Where is it pulling you?"

"I'm not sure, it's straight ahead." said the Dark Being, gesturing forwards.

"Let's check it out. Hopefully it's something cool." said the boy, walking on ahead eagerly.

The Dark Being watched his younger self walk onward with a happy stride, feeling nothing but sorrow for the boy. This was his innocence, his youth, long forgotten and buried, replaced by the psychopath that was now in primary control, just as he had been.

"Hey hurry up oldie! You're really slow."

The Dark Being followed behind the boy, they

passed by different psychedelic buildings which didn't seem to make any architectural or structural sense other than them all having doors somewhere close to ground level.

"Weird…" said the boy.

"What's the matter?"

"This place looks even more different to what I remember," said the boy, confused.

"What do you mean?"

"I dunno, it's familiar but different, like… things have moved around a lot more than usual? You know how like in some recurring dreams things are the same but they feel different and out of place?"

The Dark Being looked around closely at their surroundings.

"Wow." said the Dark Being, watching the buildings closely, noticing that they almost seemed alive in some way.

"Hey look! This one is definitely new!" shouted the boy.

The Dark Being caught up with the boy, and stood in front of a building which didn't seem much different to the others. As he got closer to the door, he noticed a familiar number written on it with blood.

"808"

He placed his hand on the bloody numbers.

"Huh? I've never seen a door with any numbers before." said the confused boy.

"I no longer feel the pull when I touch it."

The boy attempted to open the door but it was locked.

"Aw, I thought this new one might be unlocked at least."

The Dark Being looked down at the handle. It opened itself effortlessly, revealing a white void.

"**WOAH!** How did you do that?!" screamed the boy in excitement, briefly sticking his head into the white void comically.

"I assume he locked *you* out of these doors, but remember, me and *him* traded places. This body we once shared is probably the key."

"So you can probably open all of the doors right?!" shouted the boy who was having trouble controlling the volume of his voice.

"I would guess so, yes."

"We gotta open 'em all! There's so much I want to catch up on."

...

"Alex... if all of these buildings truly guard our memories, then there are some you should not see. I fear whatever is beyond this door might be one of them."

"Come on! I wanna know more about us!"

The Dark Being lowered himself to the boy's level.

"Alex, it brings me no joy to say this... We didn't turn out to be the best person."

The boy looked down and began fidgeting with the football he was still carrying.

"We never became that famous footballer we always thought we'd be," said the Dark Being, placing his hand on the football. "We never got around to owning our own island, we never did meet Sean Connery."

The boy looked up in shock.

"Aw... come on! **Really?!**"

"We never did end up winning the lottery. Instead, we used our talents for self gain and gratification, harming others in the process. Whether I like it or not, I am an evolution of *him*, *he* is my past. As much as I'd like to say he isn't me, the fact is, that was me and I did horrible things which I now deeply regret. I can't escape what we've done, but at the very least I need to shield what little innocence I have left from the things I am not proud of."

The Dark Being raised himself back to his own level, still looking at the void of white awaiting him

"I know we're not a good person…" said the boy "I saw enough to know that. Even those later memories I couldn't see, I still felt 'em when they happened." continued the boy as he walked up to Alexander and held onto his hand "I forgive you. You're doing your best. I'm glad we eventually became you, even if it took a little longer than I hoped."

The Dark Being let out a deep sigh of relief, feeling like a weight had been lifted off his shoulders. He began to realise that he had been holding onto a large amount of guilt for letting his inner child down, even after all these years.

"I appreciate that more than you'll ever know, Alex." said the Dark Being while squeezing the small hand of the boy "Okay, let's go in together then."

The boy smiled. They began walking through the door together as the void swallowed them both whole. Random memories began flashing in front of them.

"Hey listen up oldie, this sort of place can be very overwhelming, you really have to focus to see the memories otherwise they'll all play at the same time." said the boy, still holding the Dark Beings hand but a bit tighter.

"There's so much randomness." said the Dark Being.

"Think of it like a thought distracting you when you're reading a book. Your mind will wander sometimes."

The Dark Being began to focus, allowing things to become much clearer as a scene began to build around them brick by brick.

...

'Alexander' awoke, he sat up and looked around, seeing shadows dancing around the bedroom. He ran into the corner of the room and attempted to catch them, but they quickly hid behind the wardrobe.

"What are you doing?" asked Mary from their bed, rubbing her eyes.

Alexander did not respond, and instead stood still for a while staring at the wardrobe as if he was stalking prey.

"Allie, you're sleepwalking again." she said while carefully walking over and putting her hand on his shoulder "Shh, come get back in bed."

Alexander obeyed and returned to the bed, instantly falling back asleep.

...

"She's pretty." said the boy, watching the memory with the Dark Being who made no response "Are you okay?"

"Yes, it's… it's just been a while since I've seen the real her. I'll be okay."

"Do you wanna stop?"

"No, let's keep going. I have no recollection of this happening other than what Mary told me the following morning. I'd been sleepwalking a lot in the months leading up to her death. I believe this was one of the first times I had a night terror, it's very similar to how she described it happening."

Another memory began to build around them.

…

Alexander opened the door to the bedroom while holding a small plastic bag. Mary was deep asleep on her side, lightly snoring. He carefully crept towards his side of the bed and got in, turning his light on dimly. After a few moments he leaned over her and began searching for veins on her arm closest to him. After locating the most viable one, he dabbed the spot with a numbing solution. Once numbed, he took out a syringe from the same plastic bag and began injecting her with an unknown orange liquid.

After emptying the syringe into her body, he quickly began dismantling it, putting the components and numbing solution back into the plastic bag. He stood up and made his way out of the bedroom.

"Allie?"

Alexander stopped in his tracks, moving the plastic bag out of sight.

"Yes?"

"What are you doing?"

"Nothing."

"What's that bag?"

He looked at it, realising he had not concealed it from her field of view very well, he then looked at her with a vacant glance.

*"I am just getting rid of some **rubbish…**" he said with a slight smile obscured from her.*

"Okay just get back into bed, we have to be up early, remember?"

He nodded and left the room to dispose of the plastic bag.

…

"I can't believe it. We really did kill her, didn't we?"

"***You*** didn't, Alexander. ***He*** did that."

"He is me. I am him."

The boy shook his head.

"You can shake your head all you want boy, but the fact of the matter is, Alexander Lowe killed Mary Lowe." said the Dark Being raising his voice.

The boy squeezed his hand even tighter, surprising the Dark Being with his unnatural strength. He looked at the child who was laser focused on the Dark Being, with a determined look on his face.

"You stopped being him decades ago. He evolved while in confinement here into something far worse than you ever were." said the boy, again sounding more adult-like.

"But-"

"Alexander, listen to me. We think we're the same person we were yesterday, but the truth is, we're different people every single day. The human body is in a constant state of renewal, there is not a single atom in your body that was there when you were the same age as my appearance. Our neurons and our memories, however, those we do indeed share, only degraded slightly with time. That's how we learn to be better than the person we were yesterday, we cannot judge ourselves by who we are not."

"Where did you learn that?" asked the Dark Being, quite impressed with the boy's sudden statement which seemed far more mature.

"Sometimes your best therapist is yourself, Alexander."

"So it would seem…" said the Dark Being, watching similar memories playing in front of him "I suppose *he* saw Mary as the reason he was buried here. She turned me into the man I eventually became. He was right, we did suppress him, we did lock him away and rightfully so. Ever since I met Mary, I have totally changed for the better. She was everything to me but nothing but a threat to *him*…"

"Doesn't sound like the same person, does it?" asked the boy.

X

Rain hammered down onto the tarmac under the glow of the lampposts in the dead of night. Lenny leaned back against his car, which was tucked beneath the shelter of the Grosvenor bridge in central London, watching the thunderous downpour. He was accompanied by his Shadow, who stood next to him in his dark suit, wearing the silver vulture pin. Lenny took a slow drag from his cigarette, then glanced at his watch: 01:59 a.m. A dark silhouette emerged into view in the dimly lit undercarriage of the bridge, it began walking towards them both.

"It has been a *long* time, Lenny." said Alexander, finally fully emerging from the darkness into view with a smile on his face under the bridge lights.

Lenny was taken aback by Alexander's appearance. He was significantly younger than he was when he last saw him, his eyes however were very dry and bloodshot. Lenny carefully pulled out his gun and held it at his side.

"How did you find me?" asked Lenny, with his cigarette still in his mouth.

"That is not of importance right now, but rest assured that the person you were meeting with will not be coming."

Lenny cocked the hammer of his gun.

"Who are you?" asked Lenny, noticing that the odd accent he heard on the phone was now gone, replaced instead with his usual voice but with more bass to it.

"You always were straight to the point, I had nearly forgotten."

"You're acting like we haven't seen each other in a long time."

"You have no idea how right you are, *Lenny...*" said Alexander who was pacing back and forth.

...

"Leave us." instructed Lenny to his Shadow, who quickly made his way towards an SUV parked on the other side of the road under the bridge.

...

"What the fuck is going on? You look like you did in the eighties. Did you hire a plastic surgeon to hide your identity? Where is that limp of yours? What the fuck happened in that hospital with the detective?"

The two stood staring at each other, Alexander did not say a word.

...

"They're looking for you, you know?" asked Lenny.

"I am aware," said Alexander, stoically, taking a step forward.

"That's close enough," said Lenny sternly as he raised his gun and aimed it at Alexander's head.

Alexander took a step backward, acknowledging Lenny's boundaries.

"People are speculating how you, Dr. Alexander Lowe, some boring old fuck made another human being explode like a firework."

"It is quite simple really."

"Yeah?" asked Lenny, taking a final drag of his cigarette before flicking it away into the River Thames with his free hand, now placing it under the magazine of the gun for added support.

"I manipulated every atom of the detective. The atoms in his body vibrated extremely fast, rapidly heating up his entire body. ***Poof***. He was gone, handed back to the Universe for repurpose."

Lenny let out a snicker in disbelief, but Alexander's reaction was stone cold.

"Was it some sort of explosive device?"

"I just told you what happened, Lenny."

Lenny raised his eyebrow, unimpressed at the fiction he believed he was hearing.

"I do not expect you to believe me. It would be much easier if I showed you." said Alexander, reaching into his pocket.

Lenny took a step forward to Alexander with a very serious demeanour.

"Lenny, please. I mean you no harm. Besides, that gun won't do you much good against me as I am now."

"What are you on about?"

Alexander began to scout the area briefly.

"Look, if you're going to shoot me with an M1911 under a bridge, at the very least put a silencer on it for Christ sake. Let's not attract a scene. Did I not teach you anything?"

"Are you really asking me to shoot you?" asked Lenny, carefully putting a silencer on his pistol, acknowledging that if he was forced to shoot for whatever reason, it would be better silent as a shot from an M1911 is loud enough, but it would be amplified greatly with the acoustics of the bridge.

"Yes, I am. I was going to demonstrate with something far simpler but a bullet will also work just fine. Besides, being shot at would be a good experiment for any future scenarios."

"Alexander, we go way back but I will put a bullet in you if you make a sudden move. I have bigger priorities within my role." said Lenny, now aiming the pistol at Alexander's chest.

Alexander raised his left hand.

"Let's start small first, shoot my hand."

"I'll do it, you know?"

"I know you will." said Alexander as his face became very focused "***Shoot.***"

Lenny shot Alexander's hand, the bullet went right through it and down the street. Alexander groaned loudly, holding his hand close to his stomach, applying pressure from both sides as blood poured from the wound.

"I don't know what I expected… What the fuck happened to you since you left the society?" asked Lenny, bewildered at what was going on in front of him "Look, I don't have time for this. You clearly lost your fucking mind when that detective kicked your head in."

Lenny lowered the gun to his side and opened the door to his car. He whistled over to his Shadow who gave a thumbs up and got into the driver's seat of the other car across the road.

"What is the ***rush***?" asked Alexander, raising his hand up once again to show the wound quickly healing itself.

Lenny looked at Alexander in shock.

"How the fuck are you doing that?" he asked, quickly closing his car door. He once again aimed the gun at Alexander.

"Again," said Alexander, continuing to hold his hand up.

"Explain yourself!" shouted Lenny.

"AGAIN."

Lenny shot again. This time the bullet crumbled as it hit Alexander's skin.

"Holy shit…" said Lenny under his breath, lowering his gun slightly as he realised the power his gun had over Alexander was no longer present.

"**AGAIN!**" shouted an excited Alexander once more, suddenly pacing forwards like a madman at Lenny to provoke him into action.

Lenny quickly aimed the gun at Alexander's chest and shot four more times rapidly, but the same thing happened, each bullet disintegrating before his eyes as it made contact with Alexander. As he got closer, Lenny began to panic. He aimed the pistol at Alexander's head and shot, but the bullet once again crumbled. Alexander grabbed the silencer of the gun, putting it against his forehead. He looked at Lenny with an angry, but confident expression on his face.

"***Again…***" said Alexander, in a much more sinister and deeper tone, which Lenny recognised from the phone call.

Lenny shot his last bullet, but absolutely nothing happened. Alexander smiled as the gun began to fall apart in Lenny's hand, leaving only a circle indent on Alexander's head where the silencer was pushed against his skin.

"What the fuck… are you? What have you done to yourself?"

"I have achieved a human being's true potential. There is ***nothing*** I cannot do."

"What do you want from us?" asked Lenny nervously, realising that the story of this detective exploding now had a lot more merit to it.

"Do not be afraid, Lenny. I came here as a friend. I just had to demonstrate for you to believe me. As I said, I need to talk with both you and Hubert. Where is he?"

Lenny knew he couldn't let his superior anywhere near whatever Alexander had become, but his eyes deceived him as they involuntarily shifted to the SUV parked on the other side of the road. The Shadow was still watching like a hawk from the driver's seat.

"Ah… of course." said Alexander under his breath as he began walking towards the SUV.

Lenny's Shadow jumped out of the driver seat and stood between Alexander and the car.

"Stand down!" shouted Lenny.

"You heard him." said the Shadow to Alexander, carefully aiming his gun at him.

"No Keith! **You!** Stand down!" shouted Lenny, following behind Alexander at a safe distance.

Keith quickly did as he was instructed and moved aside, keeping his gun pointed at Alexander.

"Hello, Hubert." said Alexander as he opened the car door.

Hubert did not respond, clearly concerned with the scenes he had witnessed through the tinted window. Alexander took a seat across from him, and Lenny quickly jumped into the car as well, sitting beside Hubert.

"Alexander...?" asked Hubert, looking at his appearance closely with a sense of nostalgia and concern.

"It has been some time, Hubert. You are looking well as always."

Hubert looked at Lenny for answers, but he could not give any reassurance. He regained his composure and gestured to the tablet which was stuffed in a compartment behind one of the seats, which Lenny passed over to him. Hubert tapped on the screen a few times and turned it around. Alexander took the tablet and pressed the large play button.

"A manhunt is currently underway for renowned scientist, Dr. Alexander Lowe, who is wanted for suspected murder. Dr. Lowe, who lost his wife in 2014, was reportedly mentally ill before the attack, and had just woken up from coma after receiving multiple head injuries. The suspected murder, according to eyewitnesses, was impossible to explain, one man was quoted as saying 'One second the policeman was there, the next the room was red hot, the walls were caked in blood. I have no idea what happened!'. Police are asking the public to take extreme caution around Dr. Lowe, especially with the amount of unknown factors relating to what happened to the victim. Patricia Thorne, BBC News."

Hubert took the tablet back and took on a more serious tone.

"Explain yourself," said Hubert sternly.

"As I said to Lenny, it is quite simple. I boiled that detective's body from within which caused it to rapidly rupture in all directions."

...

"How?"

"When I made contact with his body, we became

connected at an atomic level. I instructed the atoms within his body to vibrate to the point where they became unstable."

Hubert squinted his eyes in both annoyance and disbelief.

"Alexander, we don't live in a supernatural world. This isn't a land of fairytales." said Hubert who was raising his voice a little "We're aware of your spending and your talents. What technology have you been cooking up in that lab of yours to accomplish these feats?"

"I thought the society rules stated that you don't ask questions?" asked Alexander playfully as Lenny and Hubert looked at each other in frustration "What I am telling you is *not* of supernatural origin, it is also not technological. It is as normal as breathing. I have harvested the automated processes of the body, which has given me the ability to control every atom within my reach. I can instruct them to do my bidding."

"You know you sound nuts, right?" asked Lenny comically, before Hubert raised his hand to hush him.

"What do you want?" asked Hubert, with a serious tone.

"I want nothing more than to be part of the society again. I have no ulterior motive."

Hubert snickered uncharacteristically.

"So, you get this 'power' and simply want to go back to your old day job? It doesn't make a lick of sense, Alexander."

Alexander leaned forwards.

"Silver controls the world, to a certain degree. Your sponsors and clients are some of the most powerful people alive today. I want to be part of that world again, I want to contribute to that, and my newfound abilities can greatly aid towards the society's ultimate goals. Speaking of which... I have some information which will greatly benefit the society and some of its sponsors."

Hubert leaned forward, meeting Alexander's gaze.

"Your tenure at the society was highly valued, Alexander. I don't think you realise how close you were to being promoted to Umbra, the same rank as me, before your sudden exit. When you left, you made things very problematic for us, especially to Lenny." said Hubert, gesturing to Lenny "Whom reported directly to you as your Shadow. Replacing people like us in our world is no easy task, especially mid operation when you took your leave."

"I can assure you, that was not *me*."

"I have to agree, when you left it was very unlike you. Whereas now, I feel like I'm talking to the old Alexander again." said Lenny, before being hushed again by Hubert.

this heat you have on you right now. We will do our part to mitigate that in the background, but your face and name are out there now as a killer, we cannot undo that."

"Then we have a deal?" asked Alexander with a smile on his face.

"Indeed." confirmed Hubert, with a clear worry on his face.

"Then, allow me to expand on the research in California. They have created nanobots, microscopic robots, that can be programmed to cure ***anything***. If you visit a doctor, they could analyse your body once and give you a bespoke cure at any point throughout your life. This could even be expanded to servicing the body, without the need to ever visit a doctor, perhaps only for updates to the nanobots medical database. You could, in theory, be eternally youthful."

"Wow." said Hubert out loud in amazement, knowing the immediate potential.

"As you can imagine, this would be a significant source of long-term income. Even on the marketing side. The team in California who invented this wishes to make it accessible to everyone for pennies. They don't want private companies to own this in any way so they are being extra cautious, which we can use against them. The ramifications of unleashing this on the world would be catastrophic to the medical industry, and by extension, our sponsors."

"Right, I want you to put your full focus on this opportunity in California. We will evaluate this new arrangement once your work there is complete."

Alexander nodded once again and looked at Lenny with a genuine smile on his face, and extended his hand.

"Just like the old days, right Lenny?"

Lenny placed his head in his hands, letting out a deep regretful growl.

"I'm nearly sixty years old… I should be planning my retirement…" he said under his breath.

…

"Fuck it… If it's anything like the old days, I'm in."

"***Oh, it will be,***" said Alexander, once again in a deeper tone.

"Just keep your hands to yourself, alright?" chuckled Lenny nervously, looking at Alexander's extended hand.

Alexander smiled while returning his hand. After they were finished with their discussion, Lenny and Alexander exited the SUV and both got into Lenny's car. They both sat there for a few moments, before Lenny plucked up the courage to ask the question that had been on his mind the entire time.

"Be real with me, Alexander. I don't buy the story you just told Hubert. Why are you really with the society again and how can I possibly contribute in any way to someone that can, apparently, do anything? Why me?"

Alexander looked down the street at the thunderous waterfall of rain in front of them, which was still illuminated by the lampposts. He was trying his best to formulate a response, something he never had a problem with prior but this was a touchy subject. The more his thoughts danced around the subject, the more difficult it became to formulate it into words. He began itching his neck in anxiety but suddenly let go, choosing full transparency.

"Lenny... I have... been in solitude... for quite some time, much longer than you probably realise. It took me a long time to find myself again, to ***resurface***. The only thing I could relate it to is being locked in a prison cell for centuries, it was an unimaginable amount of time by myself."

Lenny looked on with concern at his old friend. He noticed tears welling in Alexander's bloodshot eyes, as if he was reliving trauma. This was the old Alexander, the one he went to school with, the one who told him everything and confided in him, the older brother he never had that always looked out for him. Lenny thought back to when Alexander and Mary first got together. Their friendship took a major backseat and eroded away over time to simply business associates.

"You may not believe what I am about to tell you, Lenny, but it is the truth. That isolation was not in this world, I was trapped in my own subconscious, Hubert was right, I did have a split personality in a sense, but it is much more complicated than that. *He*, my former self, left Silver, *he* got married to that woman, *he* somehow ended up becoming a celebrity… I witnessed him trade the potential of the society for a mediocre government job and fame. You, I and the Silver were building something incredible. Lenny, our time together back in those old days… It was great, we ran this city. You are right to worry, I have no doubt I could do all of this on my own now but... Power is one thing, but I lack…-"

"Aw, you just want a friend again right?" laughed Lenny while elbowing him in the ribs.

"Oh shut the fuck up, Lenny." laughed Alexander who was caught off guard.

Alexander growled and wiped the corners of his eyes.

"I miss those days. I *crave* them, they are far more nostalgic to me than you realise. Those were the best moments of my life and the thought of returning kept me going through all of that isolation. I have not changed a bit,

"Do you have some sort of split personality, Alexander?" asked Hubert abruptly.

"That would be a good summary of what I have been through recently, however, there is nothing split about me now. I am my old self, reborn *anew*. I am whole again."

Hubert sighed while sitting backwards in his seat again. He began looking out of the window.

"So, you can destroy anything you touch?" asked Hubert, shifting the conversation back to Alexander's abilities.

"Not only that, I can create. I can do anything, essentially." said Alexander as he carefully took the tablet out of Hubert's hands.

"What is this?" asked Alexander.

Lenny tilted his head and began wondering how hard those detectives kicked Alexander's head in.

"It's a tablet, Alexander…" said Lenny, looking at it closely humorously "A Windows tablet, if you want to be specific."

"*No*. It is a collection of atoms." said Alexander as he closed his eyes and focused on the tablet "Aluminium, carbon, hydrogen, oxygen, nitrogen, silicon, copper, lithium, cobalt… and other trace elements like gold and tin."

The tablet began to transform before their very eyes,

rearranging itself as if the laws of physics no longer applied. Lenny and Hubert's eyes widened in awe at what they were witnessing. They glanced up at Alexander, who was fully focused on the tablet, with veins bulging out on the side of his head. The shape of a gun began to quickly materialise itself from the soup of atoms within Alexander's grasp.

"What. The actual. Fuck…" said Hubert, again uncharacteristically.

The gun began to assemble more visible features before finally taking on the full appearance of Lenny's M1911. He then passed it to him.

"I believe I owe you a gun," said Alexander with a smirk.

"Holy shit!" shouted Lenny, who took the gun, which was hot to the touch. He began to examine it with Hubert as Alexander continued to talk.

"Every atom is made up of protons, neutrons and electrons. They are all the same until they are clumped together and re-arranged in a certain way. I simply disassembled them, and instructed them to reassemble using my thoughts as the blueprint. What I just did is entirely possible when you unlock your mind's true potential."

"I feel like I've seen a few movies about that." joked

Lenny.

"Of course you have..." replied Alexander, unimpressed.

"Alexander, are there any limits to this ability of yours?" asked Hubert, now very interested.

"None, however, I am not here to print you money. I am asking to return to my former role within Silver." replied Alexander abruptly.

Lenny looked at Hubert, who was taking a moment to consider his options.

"Speaking of finances, as I mentioned earlier, I have something of importance to share with the society." interrupted Alexander as Hubert was mid thought.

"Oh?" asked Hubert.

"A former acquaintance of mine in California and his team have created something that will revolutionise the medical industry. Some of the society's sponsors would be very interested in this as the profits would be astronomical. We are talking about a new multi billion dollar industry that would no doubt put the sponsors out of business, however, if you took the information I hold, they could instead become the industry leaders and profit endlessly."

"Go on..." pushed Hubert further.

Alexander opened his hands and placed his palms facing upward, gesturing he wouldn't reveal more as it currently stood.

"Alright, Alexander. You forfeit the rights you previously had as a client and instead, your former membership is restored."

Lenny turned to Hubert in surprise, he did not expect such a quick answer.

"As of right now, you are demoted back to Shadow. You will report directly to-."

"Lenny. I will *only* work with him."

"Not possible. He is currently paired with Keith."

"This is my only requirement," said Alexander sternly, taking on a more serious expression.

Hubert looked at Lenny, who shrugged comically. While Lenny found this fascinating and somewhat humorous, Hubert was very nervous about all of this. He felt like a hostage to a madman that wanted to relive his younger days, and there wasn't much he could do. He had seen Lenny shoot Alexander with no effect, so he knew he was an incredibly dangerous threat, especially with law enforcement on his tail. At the same time, the lust of greed was seductive, and it overruled most of Hubert's concerns. The Alexander he knew was many things, but he rarely lied.

"Okay. We'll do this, but it will be a trial run. No guarantees. You will need to be extra cautious with all of this heat you have on you right now. We will do our part to mitigate that in the background, but your face and name are out there now as a killer, we cannot undo that."

"Then we have a deal?" asked Alexander with a smile on his face.

"Indeed." confirmed Hubert, with a clear worry on his face.

"Then, allow me to expand on the research in California. They have created nanobots, microscopic robots, that can be programmed to cure *anything*. If you visit a doctor, they could analyse your body once and give you a bespoke cure at any point throughout your life. This could even be expanded to servicing the body, without the need to ever visit a doctor, perhaps only for updates to the nanobots medical database. You could, in theory, be eternally youthful."

"Wow." said Hubert out loud in amazement, knowing the immediate potential.

"As you can imagine, this would be a significant source of long-term income. Even on the marketing side. The team in California who invented this wishes to make it accessible to everyone for pennies. They don't want private companies to own this in any way so they are being extra cautious, which we can use against them. The ramifications of unleashing this on the world would be catastrophic to the medical industry, and by extension, our sponsors."

"Right, I want you to put your full focus on this opportunity in California. We will evaluate this new arrangement once your work there is complete."

Alexander nodded once again and looked at Lenny with a genuine smile on his face, and extended his hand.

"Just like the old days, right Lenny?"

Lenny placed his head in his hands, letting out a deep regretful growl.

"I'm nearly sixty years old… I should be planning my retirement…" he said under his breath.

…

"Fuck it… If it's anything like the old days, I'm in."

"***Oh, it will be,***" said Alexander, once again in a deeper tone.

"Just keep your hands to yourself, alright?" chuckled Lenny nervously, looking at Alexander's extended hand.

Alexander smiled while returning his hand. After they were finished with their discussion, Lenny and Alexander exited the SUV and both got into Lenny's car. They both sat there for a few moments, before Lenny plucked up the courage to ask the question that had been on his mind the entire time.

"Be real with me, Alexander. I don't buy the story you just told Hubert. Why are you really with the society again and how can I possibly contribute in any way to someone that can, apparently, do anything? Why me?"

Alexander looked down the street at the thunderous waterfall of rain in front of them, which was still illuminated by the lampposts. He was trying his best to formulate a response, something he never had a problem with prior but this was a touchy subject. The more his thoughts danced around the subject, the more difficult it became to formulate it into words. He began itching his neck in anxiety but suddenly let go, choosing full transparency.

"Lenny... I have... been in solitude... for quite some time, much longer than you probably realise. It took me a long time to find myself again, to *resurface*. The only thing I could relate it to is being locked in a prison cell for centuries, it was an unimaginable amount of time by myself."

Lenny looked on with concern at his old friend. He noticed tears welling in Alexander's bloodshot eyes, as if he was reliving trauma. This was the old Alexander, the one he went to school with, the one who told him everything and confided in him, the older brother he never had that always looked out for him. Lenny thought back to when Alexander and Mary first got together. Their friendship took a major backseat and eroded away over time to simply business associates.

"You may not believe what I am about to tell you, Lenny, but it is the truth. That isolation was not in this world, I was trapped in my own subconscious, Hubert was right, I did have a split personality in a sense, but it is much more complicated than that. *He*, my former self, left Silver, *he* got married to that woman, *he* somehow ended up becoming a celebrity... I witnessed him trade the potential of the society for a mediocre government job and fame. You, I and the Silver were building something incredible. Lenny, our time together back in those old days... It was great, we ran this city. You are right to worry, I have no doubt I could do all of this on my own now but... Power is one thing, but I lack...-"

"Aw, you just want a friend again right?" laughed Lenny while elbowing him in the ribs.

"Oh shut the fuck up, Lenny." laughed Alexander who was caught off guard.

Alexander growled and wiped the corners of his eyes.

"I miss those days. I *crave* them, they are far more nostalgic to me than you realise. Those were the best moments of my life and the thought of returning kept me going through all of that isolation. I have not changed a bit,

I am the Alexander you once knew, before that *woman*. I still get my kicks out of lurking in the shadows, pulling strings. Seeing what happens if I pull too much."

Lenny watched Alexander's mannerisms closely.

"We always did make an efficient team," said Lenny "We were quite unstoppable, even for Silver's standards. Imagine what we could do now?" he pondered further.

"We can take the society to the next level, it could truly rule the world," said Alexander confidently.

"Look, Alexander, I don't know what exactly you have planned, but I'm in. I don't want to bore you with my life story, but things haven't exactly been thrilling in recent years for me either outside of the business."

Lenny extended his hand to Alexander, no longer fearful. Alexander smiled, extending his hand too.

"Let us get back to work. Just stop calling me Alexander, it is weird when you say it." said Alexander as he shook Lenny's hand.

"You got it, Champ," laughed Lenny as he started the ignition and held onto the steering wheel, still looking ahead, but not driving.

"Is something else the matter?" asked Alexander.

"I don't know how to phrase this other than... What the hell happened after your wife died?" asked Lenny abruptly.

Alexander knew if they were going to work together like old times, this continued honesty was essential.

"Do you really want to know?"

"Tell me everything, Champ," said Lenny while driving away from under the Grosvenor bridge and into the storm ahead.

Over the next hour, Alexander explained everything that led up to this moment.

"Unbelievable, but one thing I don't understand is… at what point did **you** get buried into your own subconscious?"

"It was not long after we met that *woman*. It was not an instantaneous thing either, I just… lost control slowly, and before I noticed it, my fate was already sealed. Life just got blurry over time until I wasn't here anymore, I thought it was normal with age but far from it. I lost my focus and I was replaced by a newer, inferior version of myself."

"So this other 'Alexander', the one that was around for the last thirty years, that boring whiny version I had to put up with for half my life, what happened to him when you took back control?"

Alexander looked at Lenny with a sinister smile.

"He is where he belongs. Buried. Tombed. As I was." said Alexander, tapping on the side of his head.

"Brutal." laughed Lenny.

Alexander nodded.

"Since we're being honest here, even though you look like your younger self, you look like absolute shit." said Lenny.

Alexander looked at Lenny unimpressed.

"Great, thanks Lenny." said Alexander slightly amused. "Well, that is likely because I have not slept since taking back primary control."

They stopped at a red light.

"Hold on, what? How long have you been awake?" asked Lenny, looking over at Alexander with concern.

"Just under a month."

"A month?! Are you serious? That has to be a world record."

"I am keeping the urge to sleep at bay, but it is very overwhelming even with full control over my body. Sleep is an essential process for cleansing the mind and I have not initiated it since then."

"You know you could just... sleep, right?"

Alexander looked at Lenny with disapproval.

"Absolutely not."

"Why?"

Alexander began to grow frustrated, sighing and fidgeting with his jacket.

"If I sleep, there is a risk that the *other me* will emerge again, temporarily. He might be inferior but he is me, so he is dangerous." said Alexander in frustration, "Enough of this. Let us focus on our next move. We will broach this subject when the time comes."

The light turned green and they drove off into the darkness of the night.

XI

A week had passed since Alexander met with Lenny and Hubert underneath the Grosvenor bridge. Lenny, dressed in his signature maroon suit arrived at the Cancer Treatment and Research Lab in California alongside a Silver henchman.

"Hello darling, we're here to see Dr. Steven Abel," said Lenny with a cheeky smile.

"Oh I love that accent! Are you British?"

"You've got good taste." responded Lenny as she began to laugh "We're from the Environmental Protection Agency. He'll be expecting us."

"Ah, Brian Henderson, correct?"

"Yep that's right," responded Lenny, playing it cool.

"He'll be down shortly. Please go ahead and sign in. I'll let him know you've arrived."

Lenny signed them both in.

"Thanks. Take a seat gentlemen."

"Thanks dear," said Lenny with a wink as he took a seat in the waiting area. He began flicking through the magazines on the table in front of him. The henchman was staring at the paintings on the wall, studying them carefully. The caretaker for the building walked up to the receptionist.

"Mornin', Holly."

"Heyyy Frank. How's it going today?"

"Better than yesterday, I swear if these cameras keep breaking like this I'm calling it quits." whispered the caretaker with a laugh.

"Oh not again." replied the receptionist.

The henchman and Lenny looked at each other and subtly gestured at one another in approval. After several minutes, Dr. Abel arrived in the lobby.

"Gentlemen, sorry for the delay."

"We only just got here, don't worry."

"Did Ned **finally** retire?" asked Steven comically.

"Yes, Ned retired," responded Lenny, going along with the story.

"Such a shame, he's been doing our EPA inspections for the last fifteen years. He's been talking about retiring for most of those years though!" laughed Steven.

Lenny laughed along, as the henchman watched Steven's body language carefully. They made their way into the elevator which began to rise up to the eighth floor. There was an eerie silence in the elevator and Steven noticed the other man was watching him carefully. He decided to break the awkward silence.

"So there's two of you these days?"

"Ned was very experienced and got through inspections efficiently, so they temporarily assigned the two of us to this location after his retirement."

"Makes sense, Ned was always very thorough. He never looked as smart as you guys though, he always looked like he rolled out of bed." joked Steven.

They both ignored the comment and began to put on black gloves at the same time. Steven found this odd, but didn't question it. The elevator reached the eighth floor and Steven swiped his ID card on the elevator door. As the door to the lab opened, the henchman watched as Steven returned the keycard to his left trouser pocket. He began showing the two around the lab, however the introduction was quickly cut short.

"Dr. Abel, we've had an anonymous tip-off that you've developed nanobots for medical purposes. Is that correct?" asked Lenny abruptly.

Steven looked at Lenny in surprise, before rubbing his face in frustration, letting out a slight groan.

"Dr. Lowe, right?" asked Steven, looking down at the floor in frustration "He's the only one I've shared our research with, other than Dr. Woodfine. As soon as I heard about Alexander on the news, I began worrying about things potentially getting out."

They made no response, and began to pace around the lab, each holding a small device which they'd move around each corner of the lab in search for any active recording devices.

"Are you looking for the nanobots? I can take you to them."

They continued their investigation, ignoring Steven.

…

"Who else is on your team, Dr. Abel?" asked Lenny while still focused on the surrounding area.

"My team? There's seven of us including me."

"Names."

"Why do you need their names?" asked Steven, starting to become suspicious.

"We need to interview them in connection with the nanobots." replied Lenny.

…

As Lenny was checking a corner of the lab, he pushed a stack of folders over onto the floor which were obscuring his path.

"I'm not liking where this is going, gentlem-" said

Steven before being interrupted.

"*Hush.*" whispered the henchman, who was now standing behind Steven.

Steven turned around startled, feeling a very uneasy aura coming from this man. He looked tired and a little unstable, as if he was barely holding things together.

"W-what? What is going on here? Who are you two?"

"Clear." said Lenny while looking over at the henchman.

Steven looked between the two men, but suddenly became fixated on the henchman whose face began to slowly change in front of him, morphing into a much younger but still recognisable Alexander.

"A-Alex?! W-what just… What the hell is going on here?!"

Alexander took a step in front of Steven, invading his personal space. Lenny looked on with a smile on his face, still preoccupied with something else in the corner of the room.

"You *will* provide the names of your colleagues to us, or we *will* take them by force."

"What do you want?!" asked Steven, shaking with anxiety.

"Are you deaf?!" shouted Lenny from the other side

of the lab.

"Nono… I mean… what do you want their names for?"

The room went quiet as they both stared at him with cold expressions on their faces as if two reapers had just arrived to harvest the same crop.

"Are you going to hurt them?! I'll tell you anything you want about the nanobots and our research!"

Alexander began to laugh, it was deep and wet, almost alien in nature.

"***Please…*** There is nothing *you* know that I could not easily figure out myself. I have seen enough of your work the last time my former self was here. We are not here for the nanobots. We are here for *you* and your team."

"I won't give you any names!"

"We also require information on this 'Dr. Woodfine' you have been working with." demanded Alexander.

"**Absolutely not!** I won't let you harm ANY of my colleagues!"

Alexander casually pulled out a gun and examined it closely, making Steven immediately cower down to the floor. He scurried over to the other side of the room until he reached the wall.

"Shit! Oh shit!" said a panicking Steven quietly to himself while shaking.

Alexander carefully twisted a silencer onto the end of the gun and began to slowly walk towards Steven.

"Please! Don't!"

"Woodfine and information on your colleagues. *Now*."

"I can't!"

"No. You *can*, but you choose *not* to. Even your little daughter Katie would know the difference, is that not right, *father*?" asked Alexander with a sadistic grin on his face.

"**Don't you lay a fucking finger on my family!**" shouted Steven, who quickly stood to his feet in anger and ran towards him.

Alexander pushed him back across the room into a workbench with unbelievable force, smashing some glassware onto the floor in the process. A now bloodied Steven groaned on the floor in pain as he shifted his body away from the broken glass. As he began to pull himself up away from the shards, he noticed a long knife-like piece of glass on the floor outside of the view of Alexander, which he quickly grabbed and concealed. As Alexander began walking towards Steven again, Lenny whistled from across the room. He looked over to Lenny who was holding an open folder, which revealed a staff list, with both pictures and names. Steven looked over in horror as his dread multiplied.

"Oh dear…" said Alexander while tutting to himself.

Steven's breathing became heavier and panicked, he knew he had to do something. Alexander looked at him with excitement, almost as if he was feeding off his emotions.

"***Do you feel that?*** You just became completely redundant. That pit in your stomach just got a mile deeper, ***right?***"

"P-please don't, I- I have a family." he shouted over to Lenny across the room.

Lenny, who was now wearing spectacles, was distracted with something on the computer monitor. He looked over at Steven.

"Pal, if you're looking for the good cop, he ain't here!" shouted Lenny back from across the room "We'll be paying your family a visit soon enough."

"**NO!**" shouted Steven in anger.

"There is no doubt in my mind that you shared your research with your family. ***That*** is something you will not live long enough to regret." said Alexander.

"I didn't! They're innocent! I swear if you lay a finger on them!"

"You will do ***nothing***." snapped Alexander while calmly putting his gun away.

"Wha-what happened to you after you left California,

Alex?! I thought we were friends? I invited you into my home!" shouted Steven as blood began to drip down his face from the sharp cuts to his head.

"You may be surprised to hear this, but we have never actually met. I feel that introductions are redundant at this point though as you will cease to exist in a moment."

"What are you going to do?!" asked Steven as he gripped onto the shard of glass with his bloodied hand tightly, out of sight, which caused it to bleed more.

Alexander walked over besides Steven and crouched.

"We are going to take your research and give it to one of our sponsors. *Nobody* will ever know of your accomplishments."

"I don't care about the research! My family! My colleagues!"

"*They* are a problem that *we* will *solve*…"

In an adrenaline-filled lightning quick movement, Steven stabbed the sharp piece of glass into one of the arteries within Alexander's neck, causing it to spray blood everywhere as he fell backwards. He began to gurgle and hold onto his neck instinctively. Lenny quickly stopped what he was doing and rushed over. Before he could reach them, Steven quickly jumped on top of Alexander and attempted to deliver the final blow. Alexander, still pouring blood from his neck, stopped the second strike by holding

Steven's wrist firmly in place while still on his back. Steven watched as the wound began to heal itself, leaving no sign of injury.

"What the fuck?!"

Alexander began to chuckle.

"*That was good*, no, that was *VERY* good. You actually caught me off guard there. I did not know you had it in you, *doctor*." said Alexander as he firmly gripped Steven's throat with terrifying speed and force with his free hand. He began to crush both his wrist and windpipe at the same time with superhuman-like strength. Steven dropped the shard of glass onto the floor next to them and began to let out a horrific death rattle. As he began losing consciousness, his face turned from red to blue and he fell beside Alexander who quickly mounted him like a predator catching his prey. Alexander kept his grip firmly on both his wrist and throat.

"Thank you for your contributions, on behalf of our sponsors, *Dr. Abel*."

Tears were flowing down Steven's face as his final breath left his body. The forces holding Steven's atoms together became unglued and merged into the ground beneath them, becoming a soup of different elements matching the floor's structure.

"Unbelievable…" said Lenny in amazement as

Steven's body fully liquefied into the ground.

There was no longer any evidence of Steven's existence on the floor, other than a keycard, which Alexander groggily picked up. They both walked over to the computer where Lenny had been working. Alexander looked at the screen and watched as one of Silver's specialised programs was running in the background through a bespoke device which was plugged into one of the USB ports.

"It's all here, he had full access to the closed network so we didn't have to brute force it. I've taken a full copy of everything and wiped all of the data on the servers, including their off-site backup servers." said Lenny, taking his spectacles off and putting them inside his maroon jacket.

"Addresses?"

Lenny nodded.

"Dr. Woodfine?"

Lenny shook his head.

"His whereabouts might be in the files I just extracted, if not, we'll have to get his details through *other* means," said Lenny with a slight grin.

"Let's go then," said Alexander who was seemingly a little distracted and disoriented. The blood on his clothing and skin began to fade away completely.

They both made their way to the entrance of the lab and swiped the keycard, which called the elevator up to the eighth floor. As they returned to the reception area, the receptionist was showing the caretaker a blue screen of death on her computer. She heard footsteps approaching them from the direction of the elevator, and quickly noticed Lenny's unmistakable maroon suit in her peripheral vision.

"That was quick!" she said with a laugh "Don't forget to sign yourselves out." she said while resuming the conversation with the caretaker.

Lenny walked over to the desk, and looked at the book he had signed not too long ago.

"Computer problems, darling?"

"If it's not one thing, it's another 'round here!" interjected the frustrated caretaker as the receptionist giggled.

"Could you tell me the time?" asked Lenny politely for the purposes of the log book, gesturing to the clock behind them.

The receptionist looked around at the clock.

"It's…"

Lenny put a bullet into the back of her head, then one into the caretaker's too. He grabbed the log book from the desk and put it under his arm. Alexander manoeuvred his way behind the desk and gave them both the same fate as

Steven moments prior.

"Christ, that ability of yours really saves a lot of cleanup work, you're going to make some of my henchmen redundant!" joked Lenny.

Alexander did not respond, and began to quickly stumble out of the door towards the car park, as if he was about to fall over.

"You doing okay there, Champ?" asked Lenny with concern as he caught up to him.

"I fear that the sleep deprivation will soon consume me, whether I want it to or not. The feeling is becoming overwhelming the more I use my abilities."

"Is there anything I can do?"

"I will be fine. I have a plan, but let's focus on finishing the assignment first."

Lenny helped Alexander into the passenger seat of the car. He got in himself, and noticed Alexander rocking backwards and forwards ever so slightly in his seat, still with the ever reddening bulging eyes. The black gloves on Alexander's hands crumbled to nothingness, destroying any evidence that might've been on them. He did the same to Lenny's gloves, which also dissolved into thin air.

"Let's go down the list alphabetically, who is the first one?," asked Lenny as they drove off.

XII

Within Alexander's mind, the Dark Being and the boy were walking through the streets of the Red City.

"This is probably a redundant question, but is there a way to escape this place?"

The boy looked up at him hopelessly.

"Uhm, I don't think so... you handed him primary control over us." said the boy as he looked around the buildings which were subtly breathing with life "It's pretty much a done deal, ya know? He'll never give it up now he has it again. The best we can hope for is for him to change again, and join us after he's replaced by the next version, but... he won't let that happen again."

"I feared as much. If I'd known what he was capable of, I wouldn't have agreed."

"It's okay, he's a trickster like that... I get it."

...

The Dark Being stopped in his tracks.

"Hold on, how did he take over my body previously when he walked around in my sleep? Could I also do that?"

"*No.*" said the boy abruptly.

"Why not? He didn't have primary control back then yet he still somehow achieved limited control over our body. Why couldn't I just do the same?"

"*He'd* need to sleep. That'd open a crack in this world and let him in."

The Dark Being looked up at the black clouds which were still littering the orange sky. The white cracks had been absent since the transfer of power took place.

"I see. So those cracks were an opening, a gate, so to speak."

"Yeah. You entered this world through the cracks when you would dream sometimes."

"So are you saying he hasn't slept since taking control? How long has it been since that happened, in the outside world?"

The boy looked at the sky, then in all directions, trying to gauge the time flow.

"It's hard to say, time flows… differently here."

"Yes, he said the same thing." said Alexander, realising that all three of them are ultimately very similar in their thought patterns.

"If I had to guess, at least a month, maybe two? These new clouds make it even more difficult to guess."

"Incredible… It feels like it's been years. Are you

really telling me our body hasn't slept at all in at least a month?"

"Yeah, it's been a long time."

"How did you come to that conclusion?" asked the Dark Being, looking in the same directions as the boy did.

"You'll get used to it. It was easier when you were in primary control because you'd sleep at least once a day. You had a routine, but ever since he took control it's really clouded the flow of time."

The Dark Being looked at the boy, noticing that the joy in his step had been missing throughout their entire conversation, as if he was holding something back. He squatted to his level and put his hands onto the boy's shoulders firmly, looking at him with determination.

"Alex, I need to fix this. I cannot let him get away with what he has done. Is there anything we can do? **Anything** at all?"

The boy looked down at the sandy ground, defeated, knowing that his only friend wanted to get away as soon as possible, that he was just a pawn in a larger war between the two adult Alexanders. This version of the Dark Being was much different, but he was still ultimately that same selfish guy at his core.

"Yeah... at some point he **has** to sleep. I doubt he can keep correcting his mind, it's going to screw his focus up and he'll know that. That'd be your time to take control. He'll come here… and you can go there…"

"That's it! That's how we'll end this. As soon as I take over temporarily in his sleep, I'll end it."

The boy looked up at him, unimpressed. He knew he couldn't change his mind.

"Alex?"

"What?" snapped the boy.

"I *have* to do this, he's too dangerous and he can't live for what he's done to me, to us."

"I get it… I guess."

"What's wrong, Alex?"

The boy finally snapped.

"You. HIM… *YOU*. What about *ME*?! Huh?!"

The Dark Being took a step back, as if an invisible barrier formed between them, pushing them apart slightly.

"When I was replaced by him, I accepted it. I put all my hopes and dreams for the future into the next version's hands! Which then got passed onto *you*!"

"Alex…"

"No! Shut up! This *SUCKS*! I turned out to be this 'me me me' loony that's just going to end up killing himself!" shouted the boy, seething with emotion as tears began to fall. "All I hoped for was to have some fun in this world, to do some cool stuff, to make some new friends and to play!

But no! You two push me aside, you never have fun dreams. There's nothing to do here!" said the boy motioning to the city and the desert on the horizon. He caught his breath. "Then! When **YOU** come here, all you want to do is **LEAVE?**"

The boy wiped the tears from his cheeks angrily and turned his head away while the Dark Being was still holding onto his shoulders. He looked at the boy regretfully and felt a deep sense of shame and embarrassment, not at the boy but himself. He was right. He'd let his younger self down countless times throughout their life. The youthful jolts of excitement which sparked in his brain when he'd see something nostalgic, something that would've impressed his younger self, were regularly muzzled. His inner child was always in the background judging him deep within his own mind and was constantly being let down.

"Alex…"

The boy began to cry.

"I am so sorry. I-no, *we* both let you down. You did nothing wrong, you are innocent in all of this."

The boy continued to whimper.

…

The Dark Being looked at the football which was on

the ground below them. He picked it up and handed it to the boy.

"Wanna play?" asked the Dark Being in a more upbeat tone.

The boy wiped his tears away quickly in surprise.

"YOU MEAN IT?!" shouted the boy excitedly with the biggest smile on his face.

"Yes, let's play. It's been a long time since I played football, let's see if this oldie is still any good, shall we?"

"Okay! But I'm still real mad at you though!" said the boy sniffling.

They began to play together, kicking the ball around for what felt like hours, chasing each other and hiding behind the glitchy buildings.

Outside of the subconscious, Lenny and Hubert were waiting outside of a beautiful silver and dark oak door, waiting to be let in.

"What do you think he wants?" asked Lenny.

"I reported everything that happened up the chain of command, it's no wonder that *the Magnus* himself wants to see us in person." replied Hubert.

"Have you ever met him before?"

"I've only met the previous Magnus once. He promoted me to Umbra not long after he was apparently replaced. I've heard whispers that this new Magnus is nothing like the previous one."

"I hope that's a good thing." said Lenny, showing concern "I don't think I've ever seen you sweat before, Hubert."

Hubert did not answer, and instead was watching a well dressed man approach them.

"He is ready to see you both. The door will unlock shortly." said the unknown gentleman, before leaving abruptly.

Hubert and Lenny stood up and waited by the door. After a few moments, a loud mechanism turned within the wood followed by a loud clank. They waited a few moments but nothing else happened.

"I assume it's unlocked?" asked Lenny.

They pushed open the heavy, silver encrusted double doors, and were met with a beautiful and pristine office which had a very high ceiling. A thick aroma of wood hit their nostrils, from the sheer amount of solid oak furniture that dominated the room. The walls were painted in a deep shade of green, bookshelves surrounded the edges of the office and the floor was fitted with a vibrant crimson red carpet. At the end of the long room was a dark oak desk, trimmed with silver much like the door they just entered through. In the corner of the room stood a very tall broad-shouldered man. He was wearing a royal-purple waistcoat, buttoned neatly over his shirt and matching tie. He was reading one of the books from the shelves. They arrived at the end of the desk, which was much taller than they realised when they first entered. They stood patiently, waiting to be greeted.

…

Several minutes passed. Lenny became distracted, looking around the room, noticing the absence of any seats. The man closed the book, which made an audible clap in the silent and tall room. He walked over to the desk, placed the book down and rested both of his hands on the surface, finally looking them both dead in the eyes, shifting his gaze slowly back and forth between them, not saying a word.

…

"It's-" said Hubert, but before he could utter another word, the man raised his hand.

"Did your mother not teach you any manners?" asked Magnus, with a velvety and deep Irish accent.

Hubert looked at him, a little lost, like a child sent to the headteacher's office.

"Introduce yourselves," he continued.

"Lenny. Rank Shade." he said eagerly.

"Leonard?"

"Yes. Leonard Wolfe."

The man looked impressively at Lenny.

"A powerful name, I like it. Germanic?"

"Yes, grandparents."

"I thought so."

"And what about you?" asked the man, turning his gaze to Hubert.

"Hubert Smith, rank Umbra."

Magnus smirked at Hubert, as if he already knew all about him, but just wanted to see how he conducted himself.

"Very interesting indeed. I've always been fascinated with surnames, they can tell a lot about a person, their upbringing and their family. Everyone should hold loyalty to their surname and honour its origin. It's the ultimate show of respect for our lineage. Smiths are hard-working, reliable and on time." said Magnus to Hubert as he shifted his eyes to Lenny "I've only met several Wolfe's, they're often eager, brazen and a little cunning." said Magnus as he briefly narrowed his eyes slightly at Lenny.

The two did not reply, not knowing what to say or when to speak. The man appreciated the silence and continued.

"These days, I am simply known as **Magnus**."

"Latin for great, or powerful." said Lenny, suddenly.

Hubert looked to Lenny in disapproval at the interjection. Magnus smirked at Lenny briefly.

"Magnus is but a rank, a title, one passed on. In our world, my real name matters not, as it reveals a lot." said Magnus poetically, lowering his head slightly to Lenny for acknowledgement.

Lenny nodded.

Magnus raised his head and calmly drew a large breath.

"I summoned you both based on Mr. Smith here's intel. Recruiting a wanted criminal, regardless of their previous tenure, is not a smart move on the surface…" he said while tapping the desk softly with his left hand, which made audible knocks from the silver ring on his finger "I wanted to meet the trusted veterans of our wonderful society that were responsible for this… in an endeavour of understanding." said Magnus, slowly opening the palm of the same hand in a universal gesture of encouragement for them to speak.

"Alexander was one of the society's Shades for many years. He was close to the title of Umbra before he left abruptly."

"Mr. Smith, you're telling me what I already know. I want to know that which I don't."

Hubert cleared his throat nervously.

"As my report states, he will be a great asset to the society once again, he has achieved great powers through scientifi-"

"Powers, powers... you are talking about... superpowers, correct?" interrupted Magnus.

"Yes, as ridiculous as it ma-"

"Interesting, so what you wrote in your report was not in error?" asked Magnus, analysing Hubert's body language and facial expressions.

"Yes." said Hubert, surprised at the quickness of acceptance from such a crazy suggestion.

"You truly have that blacksmith spirit, Mr. Smith." said Magnus, pausing briefly, looking up at the ceiling before looking to Lenny "You will keep an eye on Dr. Lowe. Eliminate him immediately if he does anything that is counter-intuitive to our goals. He sounds like a powerful weapon that if mishandled, could cause us great harm. That leash must be kept tight at all times."

"Yes Sir." replied Lenny.

"We will make sure to-" said Hubert before being interrupted by Magnus again.

"Mr. Smith, y-"

"It's rude to interrupt, Magnus. Did your mother also not teach you any manners?" asked Lenny to the absolute horror of Hubert whose body filled with adrenaline instinctively.

...

Magnus stared a hole through Lenny, whose confidence began to crumble piece by piece as each agonising second of silence passed by.

"**Brazen.**" said Magnus with a smile "I was hoping you would call me out for my hypocrisy. You truly live up to your name, and someday you'll make a good Umbra yourself, Mr. Wolfe."

Internally, Hubert was finished with these mind games. He wanted to get out of this meeting as soon as possible, while Lenny on the other hand was smiling ear to ear at the brownie points he had earned himself.

"I am looking forward to the outcome of your operation, I hear it's nearing completion?"

"Alexander and I are eliminating anyone tied to the research, although we are having trouble locating one individual, a Dr. Woodfine, who is our last target."

"I read that in Mr. Smith here's report, he doesn't seem to be on the team itself, and is loosely affiliated with them, correct?"

"Mostly, yes. He is the one primarily responsible for the origin of the technology itself." said Lenny confidently.

"Then there is nothing to worry about, is there?" asked Magnus rhetorically as he paused for a moment "I want you both to meet with one of our sponsors from the medical world, and if they are onboard, we'll lock this research up behind iron clad patents. This mysterious doctor will be of no concern, and if he reveals himself, he will be quickly eliminated."

Hubert and Lenny nodded in agreement.

"It was a pleasure, gentlemen." said Magnus while taking his hands off the desk. He then gestured for them to leave.

Hubert and Lenny left the room and closed the heavy doors behind them which made a similar clank as before.

"How much did you tell him about Alexander in your report?" quizzed Lenny.

"Enough to convince Magnus that this is a worthwhile endeavour."

"We couldn't eliminate Alexander, even if we wanted to."

"We must pray that what Alexander has told us is truthful and hope that he really does wish to contribute to our cause again."

"I truly believe he does."

"Time will tell," said Hubert hopefully.

"He didn't even bat an eyelid at the fact Alexander has superpowers, what was that about?"

"The Magnus within the society has always had a reputation for being privy to the most secretive of knowledge that the world has to offer. It wouldn't surprise me if he's heard of something just as unbelievable before."

"Interesting…" pondered Lenny as they were walking away. Hubert gave him a look as if he should not be asking any more questions on the subject.

"How is the mitigation of Alexander's crimes going?" asked Lenny, changing subject.

"The news outlets have been silenced, and their wording has been altered. The authorities have also been advised to turn a blind eye. The heat is dying down slowly." said Hubert.

"The public will forget, as they always do," said Lenny.

Within Alexander's subconscious, the Dark Being and the boy were still playing within the Red City.

"Aw, come on! You found me again, you're too good at this!" shouted the boy who was breathing heavily.

They both sat down on the floor, looking into the

distance.

"You know what I miss most about the outside world?" asked the boy.

"Go on…"

"The sky, nature, you know? This place is my home now, but I really miss the sky, the real one, it was ***soooo*** blue."

"It was indeed beautiful, I feel like I took it for granted." replied the Dark Being.

Suddenly, the ground rumbled and loud creaking sounds could be heard all around them.

"Oh no…" said the boy looking up with concern.

"What is it?" asked the Dark Being.

"It's… ***him***… he's falling asleep."

The Dark Being turned to the sky as well, preparing himself for whatever was about to happen. The dark clouds and the sky itself began to slowly crack open as white light erupted from the seams, lighting up the desert briefly. An intense heat hit them and a light dust storm began blowing between the buildings. The boy looked at the Dark Being in terror.

"You need to go! Quick! Before he arrives!"

"What about you?"

The boy pointed into the distance with urgency, where white cracks were covering both the ground and some of the buildings, as if they were all connected.

"Just go through the cracks! Go! Quick!" shouted the boy erratically.

The Dark Being hurried into the distance towards the white cracks covering the ground. The boy looked up at the dark clouds as they began to slowly circle the city. They began to make haunting and deeper creaking noises in all directions.

The boy began to pant in fear.

XIII

Alexander awoke, still engulfed in the same white light from the crack in the subconscious that he had just passed through, or so he thought. As the intense light cleared, he became very alert to his surroundings. He found himself lying on a white padded floor, wearing some form of protection to secure his head. The air was very cold but most alarmingly, he could not move anything but his head. As he looked down, he finally noticed the tight straight jacket he was buckled into which was covered in the same red sand from the desert.

"Fuck..." said Alexander under his breath in defeat, quickly realising the situation he was in.

He scanned the small room which was covered with the same padding from the floor, other than a television and a pane of thick glass. Behind the glass stood Lenny who was staring at him and seemed concerned at the red sand that seemingly appeared from nowhere.

"Lenny?!" shouted Alexander in surprise.

Lenny shifted his gaze from the sand and pointed a remote control at the television on the wall.

"What are you doing here?" asked Alexander.

The television turned on. Lenny changed the source to USB and selected a file. A video began to play.

...

"Hello again, Secondary."

Alexander's eyes widened in fear, his first reaction was to question when this was recorded, as the Alexander on the screen was significantly younger than he was before the transfer of power. While he recognised his physical form, the eyes and mannerisms of this Alexander told another story.

*"I hope you have been having fun in **my** subconscious. There is not much to do there, other than rot, is there?"* he said spitefully *"I anticipated that you would try to escape while I slept. I know all too well how alluring that is. I want you to know that any time I sleep and you decide to intrude, you will be simply exchanging one prison for another. I will not let you meddle in my rebirth, not after all I did to get back here."*

As the video continued to play, Alexander looked at Lenny in the window with alarm.

"Lenny! You *cannot* trust this maniac. He isn't what he says he is! He'll kill you the moment you get in his way!"

Lenny ignored him and pointed at the screen.

*"the way... So, I advise you to get comfortable in that tomb of a red desert, because you will be spending a **significantly** longer time there than I did. I will-"*

"Lenny, please, he can't hear us right now, it's just me and you. Talk to me!" begged Alexander as the video continued to play.

Lenny paused the video and made his way through a hidden padded door behind Alexander. He grabbed him by one of the straight jacket's belts which caused more of the sand to fall to the ground. Lenny pointed at the paused picture of Alexander on the television.

"Listen to me very carefully. The person on that screen is someone I consider my brother, my best friend, someone I thought I'd lost many years ago. When you went off on your own ventures, you didn't just abandon him, and his ideals, you abandoned our friendship and the pact we made as kids, **remember?**" said Lenny angrily. "We've known each other almost all of our lives and you decided to let that wither away. You have no idea how much I can't stand this version of you and what you turned out to be. You whiny little bitch. Don't talk to me about ***HIM*** not being who he says he is. ***YOU*** are not who you really are!" shouted Lenny, letting go of the belt and pushing Alexander to the floor "Now, watch the rest, there's only a little bit left."

Alexander was shaken by the harsh words of his former friend. He knew that he was right about a lot of what he said, but he was also deluded, and wrapped around his alter ego's finger. Lenny resumed the video and stood behind Alexander, continuing to watch as well.

*"... consume you from within over time. Make no mistake about it, I am in full control of our body and our situation. I know you have most likely been talking to **that** childish apparition. That will cease from now on. As you are listening to this, **I** will have been alone with him for a significant amount of time."* chuckled Alexander.

"No..." whimpered Alexander under his breath.

"Every time you come back here from now on, Lenny will keep you awake long enough to give me some alone time with our younger self, then he will send you back to the desert while I resume my slumber outside of that place." chuckled Alexander one last time as the video ended.

For the next hour, Alexander lay on the padded floor, far too alert to even consider sleeping. Lenny would sometimes check in on him through the window, making sure he was awake. As the hour hit, Lenny's watch began to beep. He walked into the padded room and took the headgear off Alexander.

"Don't come back here, understood?" instructed Lenny.

Alexander did not reply.

"I'm going to need a verbal confirmation." pushed Lenny.

"We'll see, won't we? But, if I did return, I'd make sure that you're the one in this situation, not me." said Alexander eerily.

Lenny struck Alexander over the head with a baton, knocking him out cold.

He quickly opened his eyes, finding himself once again partially buried under the sand. He pushed himself upwards and checked his surroundings, not knowing how much time had passed. He then looked down at himself, noticing he was once again in the dark body he had become accustomed to.

"Alex? Are you here?" asked the Dark Being, calling out to the desert while holding the back of his head in pain.

The white cracks above him retreated through the thick black clouds as his surroundings became more dimly lit and cooler.

"Alex?"

...

He looked at the horizon and noticed he was now on the outskirts of the Red City. The city itself looked very different, and there were fewer skyscraper-like buildings on the skyline now. He quickly hurried over to the city entrance and to the area they were playing in before the white cracks opened.

"ALEX? Where are you?"

He continued to look around but saw no sign of the boy, but it was evident that something had torn through the city. The buildings were partially destroyed, including the doors which were all smashed to pieces. Door handles and broken wood littered the city, similar to when he first laid his eyes on this world. As he wandered around, looking upon the destruction, he noticed a small hand emerging from a pile of sand on a street corner.

"**Alex!**" shouted the Dark Being while rushing over to the sand pile. He quickly pulled the boy out of the heap.

As he picked the boy up, he was horrified at the brutality he saw all over his dark body. If these injuries had been sustained by anyone outside of this world, they would've been long dead.

"Alex... Christ. I'm so sorry for leaving you." he said to the near motionless boy, who was a bloodied mess.

He then noticed that the fingers on the boy's left hand were badly broken. His right hand was tightly holding onto the now deflated and cut open football. The boy barely managed to open his swollen eyes. The Dark Being covered his mouth at the horrific sight.

"D-don-don't worr-y. I'll be okay." said the boy faintly with a slight lisp.

"Please don't talk, Alex. Just stay still." he said, knowing there was absolutely nothing he could do to help him in the barren wasteland that surrounded them. He held the boy very close to himself.

"I've… had worse… I'll recover… soon." muffled the boy into the Dark Being's embrace.

The Dark Being recalled back to when he was told by his alter ego that he could not die in this world. It was clearly true with what he was witnessing.

"Did you … get out, Alexander?" asked the boy.

"Yes… But he prepared for it… he saw it coming."

The boy closed his eyes, letting out a soft sigh.

"Figures…" he exhaled.

"Please rest for now, Alex. We'll figure this out when you're better."

As the Dark Being looked into the distance, he noticed there was a single solitary door frame remaining in the city, one that he had not seen previously. It was open with the same bright light as before. The building was pristine compared to the others, with only the door missing, which was on the ground not too far from it. Not only could he feel it calling out to him, but he could hear faint haunting laughs emanating from inside it. He looked back at the boy on the floor.

"I'll be back in a moment, okay?"

"No." said the boy, pushing his weak body into the Dark Being "Take me with you… please."

The boy seemed both curious and terrified, clearly not wanting to be left alone. He partially opened his eyes again and saw the opened door for himself.

"Okay, but I don't know what to expect though. He clearly left that door here on purpose, it's likely a message… but we'll deal with it together, okay?"

The boy nodded with a faint smile on his face. The Dark Being picked him up and carried him over to the building. He passed by the door on the ground, which had the same '**808**' written on it in blood as he had seen multiple times previously. They entered the white light, triggering a memory which began to build around them.

The memory of Alexander and Lenny's visit to Dr. Steven Abel began to play out before them, revealing the brutal murders of not only him, but all of Steven's colleagues over the course of several days. After each murder, his alter ego would appear smiling at himself in a mirror at a different location, usually with blood stained clothing. Each time it happened, he'd tick off a name, until there was only one left… Dr. Woodfine. The memory replayed itself again, looping infinitely.

"What did he do this time?" asked the boy who could not focus on the erratic memories playing around them in his current state.

The Dark Being looked on hopelessly.

"Steven…"

Alexander's haunting laughs could be heard around them in the memory. The boy slowly sat himself up a little, noticing the sadness in Alexander's voice.

"Did he hurt one of your friends?"

"He killed him… he's also taken the research from my memories. He's going to give it to Silver."

Alexander's haunting laughs continued in the background of the memory.

"Silver?" asked the boy, confused and dazed still.

The Dark Being looked down at the boy regretfully.

"Like I said before, we made a lot of mistakes in our early life, and joining those lunatics was our greatest. It turned not only us into a monster, but our best friend Lenny as well. Mary made me see the light again inadvertently when we got together. She helped me see what was right, what really mattered. She even led me back to my true passion, science."

"Science is so cool..." said the boy with a bit of excitement in his croaky voice.

"Indeed, but it can also be used to create horrors. I imagine Silver will be extremely happy with this, as it will no doubt become a multi billion dollar industry for their sponsors. The way *he* looked at himself in the mirror, the way he destroyed all of the other doors in this city, leaving behind only this one, he's taunting me."

"**Wait!**" shouted the boy, quickly becoming far more alert "There's no other doors?!"

"I'm afraid not, Alex. From what I can tell when I returned, he destroyed all of them apart from this one."

"No!" he erupted, squirming in pain "I wanted to explore 'em with you!"

The Dark Being nodded in agreement.

"It would've been nice to explore the... nicer memories together... it's not looking good though." said the Dark Being to the upset boy.

As they went to exit the memory, a new one suddenly flashed all around them, showing Steven's family being brutally murdered with a haunting laugh echoing in the background. The memory shook the Dark Being to his core, but he kept up a steady pace, not wanting to see the finer details. As they exited the memory, the white light faded behind them leaving the building without an entrance.

"Can you at least tell me some good stories about us? Maybe about you and your wife? I'd like that." asked the boy.

"Of course, Alex."

The boy smiled with excitement, but was clearly still in significant pain.

"One thing's for sure though, Alex, it's far too dangerous to switch places with him again, he's made it extremely clear what the consequences of that would be." he said, looking at the boy's injuries "I promise, I'll somehow find a way to end this suffering. It's clear that even if we escaped, we'd be trading places forever and making things even worse. We **must** find a way to kill ourselves, and somehow from within this world instead."

"Please-" said the boy, reaching out.

"I'm sorry Alex, we *have* to do this. I'm sorry, I wish there w-"

The boy moved his hand from the deflated football, which dropped onto the sandy street below them, moving it onto the Dark Being's hand instead.

"Please… I want this to end too…" begged the boy

with tears flowing down his disfigured face, mixing with the blood.

The Dark Being felt a chill overcome his body, which spread throughout the streets of the city. His inner child had just begged him to kill themselves. There was no disagreement, they were in total sync, and the heavy decision had been made at that very moment by Alexander's entire subconscious. He nodded sombrely at the child and suddenly became aware of something he hadn't felt in a long time.

"Do you feel that?" asked the Dark Being to the boy.

"Follow it." instructed the boy, as gravity from an unknown origin began to pull them once again in a new direction.

"Could it be *him* messing with us?" asked the Dark Being rhetorically as he also picked up the deflated football.

"No. Let's go." the boy instructed again, uncharacteristically stern.

The Dark Being began to make his way out of the Red City and back into the plains of the desert, holding his younger self in his arms. He looked back at the city as it began to fade into a red haze, feeling like he might not lay his eyes upon it again.

After walking for a considerable amount of time, the boy wriggled free from the Dark Being's protective grasp and stood himself up. He looked up to the Dark Being with a joyful smile, no longer showing any sign of injury.

"You're okay?" asked the Dark Being.

"Told ya, it doesn't take too long to recover, I just needed a bit of time." responded the boy, holding onto his battered football eagerly.

"Impressive."

"Do you hear that?" asked the boy suddenly.

"Hear what?"

"Shh!" snapped the boy.

The Dark Being listened closely, only hearing the faint breeze in the air. He shook his head at the boy.

"Oh come on, really?!"

"I cannot hear whatever it is you're hearing, Alex."

"You can't hear those faint whispers? They're beautiful, like a harmony. I've heard 'em before, but I've never been able to figure out what they're saying though."

The Dark Being listened a bit closer, finally hearing something, but it was extremely faint.

"Is it coming from the same direction as this pull?" asked the Dark Being.

The boy nodded.

"Yep, you got it." said the boy.

"What do you know about this, Alex?"

The boy smiled at him once again, putting the football on the floor and kicked it in the direction of the gravitational pull.

As they made their way through the desert, the whispers began materialising physically as faint white wisps, weaving around them, as if they were alive and examining them both carefully. They swirled around the boy and moved through his body with ease as if he wasn't solid.

"Alex?"

"Follow." instructed the boy, gesturing ahead to a sandstorm brewing in the distance.

They pushed on through the harsh storm, which felt like it was negatively repelling them away. In a split second, the Dark Being lost the boy, who vanished onwards.

"Alex? **Can you hear me?!**" shouted the Dark Being, but the storm was deafening.

As he continued to push through to the eye of the storm, the negative repel dissipated. The Dark Being found himself in the presence of some very impressive ancient looking ruins of an old forgotten temple. He looked upon parts of the tall structure, feeling nostalgic, as if he had somehow been here before. He continued on into the ruins, passing by giant pillars on either side of him. As he came to the middle of the structure, he noticed the boy, who was still holding his re-inflated football.

"If you're going to end this, Alexander. ***This*** would be the place to do it." said the boy.

"What is this place?"

"This is my home. We're at the centre of this world. I built this place, it's where our abilities are at our strongest." said the boy while walking around the ruins, admiring his work.

…

"Who are you?" asked the Dark Being, noticing a difference in demeanour.

"We have already had our introductions, Alexander. I am the same boy you've been conversing with. Just a little more honest now." said the boy regretfully. "I am what little is left of our hopes, our dreams, our optimism, our impulse. I am the very foundation of our soul, the closest thing to the 'real' Alexander, without any shame from adulthood. Our excitable and determined inner child."

"How many of 'me' are there?" asked the Dark Being bluntly.

"There is, and has always been, the three of us.

Different versions of the same entity. Make no mistake about it, you have always been talking to yourself throughout this journey." explained the child.

A warm calming feeling washed over the Dark Being's body suddenly.

"It was you…" said the Dark Being "You were the embrace after those detectives beat me down, I felt it, and I feel it again now."

The boy nodded and looked around the temple's walls and pillars.

"Alexander… I previously called you selfish, but I'm just the same… Because we *are* the same person. I held onto you here as long as I could, but I now know that you're right about all of this…"

The Dark Being's attention was also caught by the temple walls, which were decorated with carvings of memories from different moments in their life.

"While you might not think it, you are the best of us, Alexander. You balance us, you are our **equilibrium** between *my* joy and *his* rage. I think it's only right that you, the most level headed of us, decide what happens next. We both agree though, this has to end, once and for all."

The Dark Being stood beside the child.

"It's time for you to improve, as *he* did," said the boy. "There's nothing stopping you from becoming stronger here, Alexander."

"*He* said something similar, about wanting to improve in this world."

"Indeed, *he* was building your trust. What he was teaching you though was very real. Mary wasn't an illusion of his invention like you suspected. You really did materialise her in this world, I saw it all from a distance."

"But it wasn't *really* her."

"You're right, but you still made her appear, didn't you? You did that, all by yourself. What I'm saying is, *you* also have the ability to control this world."

The Dark Being placed his hands over one of the carvings, which detailed his marriage to Mary.

"I must confess, Alexander," said the boy. "I have already seen most of our memories. I just… wanted to experience and re-live the good ones with you. Sorry for misleading you."

The Dark Being noticed the imperfections of the carvings and the childish doodles which matched his own when he was a boy.

"You carved all of this out?" asked the Dark Being in surprise.

"Yeah! Do you like it?!" asked the boy eagerly, before quickly composing himself again.

The Dark Being looked at the boy with

disappointment.

"**Hey**, why are you pushing down your excitement? Don't do that, that's how we got into this situation in the first place, remember?" asked the Dark Being sternly as the boy looked up in wonder "Your youthful joy still burns deep within us, please, never extinguish it. We'll **always** need that. Okay?"

The boy nodded as if he had just been schooled by a loving parent. The Dark Being once again looked back at all of the carvings on the walls.

"You're incredible, Alex. It's dawning on me just how long you've been stuck here."

The boy nodded with a sombre expression.

"You're just as smart and brilliant as *him* and I." said the boy "Even more so. There's just one thing holding you back."

The Dark Being exhaled as Mary's happy face flashed into his mind, which the boy also saw.

"She meant a lot to you."

"She did." replied the Dark Being.

"I think some closure is needed before we finish our story, don'tcha think?" asked the boy.

The Dark Being could feel a sudden familiar presence behind him, which rattled him to his core.

"Allie?" asked Mary.

…

The Dark Being slowly turned around. His beloved wife Mary was standing before him once again. She linked her arm to his and held onto it tightly.

"I missed you…" said Mary lovingly, rubbing his arm.

The Dark Being looked at her suspiciously, and then at the boy, who was smiling happily.

"You're right to be wary, but don't worry, *he* isn't here this time." said Mary, tightening her grip.

He once again glanced at the boy, looking for answers, who simply nodded with encouragement.

"Mary…?" asked the Dark Being in shock.

She looked at him with hope in her eyes as she glitched in and out of reality, switching between her normal appearance to how she looked after she died. The boy held the Dark Being's hand and gave him a further encouraging look.

"Allie, I'm sorry for leaving you so soon… We had a lot more planned for our future, didn't we?" asked Mary.

The Dark Being became super alert, he could feel it, **this was it**, this was the goodbye he had dreaded and avoided while she was in the hospital, the one he could under no circumstances say out loud as it would've meant acceptance of her fate.

"Allie, I'm sorry. For everything. For getting sick…"

"Mary… no… It was me who put you in that position… well, no, the *other* me… I suppose…"

The boy's grip on the Dark Being's hand tightened.

"Hey…" said the boy "You know she wouldn't blame you. She knew *you* loved her. This guilt you're holding onto, it'll only hold you back."

"Hold me back?" asked the Dark Being.

"Forgive yourself, Alexander." said the boy as he also linked his arm, mimicking Mary on the other side "*You* always did what you thought was right."

The Dark Being looked at Mary once again, who now looked identical to her younger self when they first met. She had the same smile as she did on their wedding day, full of joy, trust and hope for the future. The Dark Being's heart skipped a beat and he began to feel strange all over. He looked at his jet black hand which was beginning to crack, exposing the skin underneath. The white wisps reappeared and began to examine him closely. He looked at her with tears welling in the corner of his eyes.

"I… don't want to say goodbye."

Mary began to feel the same overwhelming sadness

overcome her.

"We might not have another chance to see each other again, Allie. Would you rather we never said goodbye?"

"I don't believe that. Not anymore, at least. I've never been the religious type, but knowing what I know now, seeing what I've seen… it wouldn't surprise me if I awoke one more time after finishing this."

"Let's hope you're right, eh?" she said while smirking, as if she knew something he didn't.

The white wisps began encircling him and Mary.

"Thank you, Mary…for being the best person I've ever known, for turning me into the man I am, for giving me hope and a purpose in life outside of my own selfish desires. For pulling me out of that deep dark depression which had consumed my life for so many of my younger years."

"Thank you for being *you*, Alexander. I'm so, so proud of you." said Mary, no longer looking upon the Dark Being, but Alexander himself.

They exchanged a kiss. Mary began to fade away with the wisps into the orange sky above them. The boy looked at one of the carvings on the walls of the temple, which depicted their wedding day kiss. He smiled. Alexander wiped the tears that had been building in his eyes and turned to the boy.

...

The boy looked at him in terror.

"D-dad?" asked the boy in fear as he took a step backwards.

"I look a lot like him, don't I?" asked Alexander, touching the scar on his face.

The boy nodded uncomfortably.

"I got that a lot in my later life, from people who knew our father. I'm reminded of him every time I look in the mirror unfortunately."

The boy pushed through his worries and stood next to Alexander, who patted the boy's head in a comforting gesture.

"Let's plan our next move." said Alexander, clearing his throat and taking a seat on the cold floor of the ruins.

The boy took a seat next to him, holding onto the football with a smile.

"Let's do this." said the equally determined boy.

XIV

The boy and Alexander were brainstorming and exchanging ideas for what felt like days. Alexander was holding onto a piece of the temple rubble, putting all of his focus onto it. The boy was carving out the last interaction between Alexander and Mary onto one of the walls.

"What about severing the brain stem?" asked the boy while breaking the silence and his own concentration. He turned around to Alexander "When you two spoke, that was something he said he could do, right?"

"He could not manipulate the atoms of our body while he was here from what I could tell. His abilities were confined to this world until I gave him primary control, after which he could do as he pleased. Besides, even if I found a way to somehow control our body, he'd probably be on high alert. It needs to be much more instantaneous, something he hasn't considered yet, something that extends from here to the outside world."

"Well, these places are connected. So maybe you could do something that would boil to the surface?"

"Yes, we're thinking along the same lines." replied Alexander, as he watched the rubble crumble to smaller pieces in his hands.

"Hey you did it!" shouted the boy as he sat besides Alexander.

"No, I wasn't trying to make it crumble."

"Oh… then what are you trying to do exactly?"

"Annihilation." replied Alexander, picking up one of the smaller pieces of rubble, putting his full focus back onto it.

"Ohhh! How does that work?!" shouted the boy eagerly.

Alexander's concentration broke, and his gaze shifted to the boy.

"Sorry… I'll be quiet."

"Don't apologise for being curious. That's a weakness that will only serve to handicap you."

The boy nodded enthusiastically.

"$E = mc^2$" said Alexander.

"Huh?"

"You asked how it works." replied Alexander.

"Oh, that's the Einstein equation, right?" asked the boy with curiosity.

"Yes, one of his many equations. He published his special theory of relativity in 1905 which changed the world. It showed that **m**ass could be turned into **E**nergy. The c^2 part is the speed of light squared," said Alexander, as the boy tried to follow. "The speed of light is an unbelievable number. If you multiply even a tiny bit of mass by that number…" Alexander paused and held up the small piece of rubble "The energy output would be enormous. Take this small piece of rubble for example, it is matter, therefore it has **m**ass. It could, under the right conditions, be converted into pure Energy, times the speed of light, squared."

"Turning something physical into energy, isn't that like an explosion? So this rock could become a grenade?"

Alexander looked at the boy with a nervous smile.

"Alex, this small piece of rubble has the potential to be turned into an explosion larger than an atomic bomb."

"Woah hey **hey!**" said the boy standing up suddenly "Don't blow us up!"

"I thought you wanted this to end?" asked Alexander with a playful smirk on his face.

"**Are you crazy?** At least give me some warning or something before you try! Besides, we've never had an *atomic bomb* detonated here! I don't know what that'll do!"

Alexander laughed at the boy's alarm, who was staring at him unimpressed with his arms folded.

"Even a single grain of sand in this world could level an entire street if it was turned into energy. This isn't science fiction, Alex, it's basic science nowadays.

Unfortunately though… I doubt it'd make a dent. I doubt *__he'd__* even notice."

"Then why are we talking about it?!" snapped the boy who was still nervous about the thought of randomly blowing up mid conversation.

Alexander passed the small piece of rubble to the boy, who reluctantly took it, as if it was a deadly weapon. Alexander then patted the ground below them.

"If we attempted this, we'd have to go big. A chain reaction that even *he* can't stop."

The boy's eyes widened as he realised what he was proposing.

"Wait, you're going to blow up… ***everything***?"

"Yes. I will turn this entire world, everything it touches, including our body… into energy."

The boy let out a loud anxious sigh as his legs wobbled below him, causing him to sit down again.

"Oh boy… this is really happening, isn't it? Okay… Well, it sounds like the only suggestion so far that might actually work. It sounds really big though… if a small rock could be converted into a blast like an atomic bomb, then our *entire* body would…"

"Eradicate everything for miles in all directions. It would be **significantly** larger."

"Could you do it?"

"I don't know, and I don't really like it. We'd have to avoid as many casualties as possible if we did try it. That alone would be very difficult considering the potential scale of the explosion... I'll need your help, Alex."

The boy's face lit up with eagerness.

Meanwhile, in the outside world, Alexander and Lenny were walking side by side on the tarmac of a private airport.

"I've been meaning to ask, why do you still wear that wedding ring?" asked Lenny curiously.

Alexander looked at it briefly.

"This is just a little trophy, a reminder of how I surfaced."

"Shit..." replied Lenny in disbelief comically as he shook his head, not expecting such a dark response.

They continued walking and met up with Hubert who was waiting next to the stairs leading to his private jet.

"Is it done?" asked Hubert.

"Yes, no traces of the research remain. Everyone that was linked with the research, other than Dr. Woodfine, has been eviscerated." replied Lenny.

Hubert looked at Alexander, then back at Lenny.

"Good news." said Hubert with a smile "As mentioned on the phone, one of the sponsors is onboard, he has some questions for you specifically, Alexander."

Alexander nodded in acknowledgment and they made their way onto the aircraft. As they passed through a curtain, Alexander locked eyes with the sponsor, who was short, balding, well dressed, very overweight and had thick prescription glasses.

"Gentlemen, this is Mr. Dean, he is the CEO of Vettol, the number one provider of medical equipment and medicine globally," said Hubert.

Mr. Dean reached out and shook both of their hands. As he shook Alexander's, he felt dread, as if something sinister was reaching out to his soul and examining him closely, but he quickly brushed it off as heartburn. Hubert watched the interaction carefully, trying to gauge Alexander's thoughts but to no avail. They all took a seat.

"Mr. Lowe, From-"

"Doctor, Lowe." replied Alexander sternly.

"Yes, yes." replied the CEO unamused "From what I could gather from our mutual friend Hubert, you have a new product idea that you think would be suitable for our portfolio?"

"Mr. Dean, there would be no addition. This ***would*** be your portfolio. Your existing products would become obsolete overnight. We are talking about redefining your ***entire*** industry."

An attractive airhostess entered the passenger lounge,

which grabbed Lenny's full attention.

"We'll be taking off shortly, gentlemen. Please fasten your seatbelts and put any large items away until we're in the air." she said nervously with a side glance at Lenny, who she had unfortunately met before on previous flights.

As she turned away to leave, Lenny began making crude facial expressions to Hubert.

"Some things never change, do they Lenny?" asked Alexander, chuckling to himself.

"He's even worse nowadays from what I've been told, if you can imagine." piped up Hubert, laughing along.

As the airhostess walked to the other side of the plane to get something, Lenny placed his hand on her thigh and pulled her down onto his lap as she gasped. He took out a cigar from a silver case concealed in his jacket pocket with his free hand.

"Care to help me out, dear?" he said as he aimed the cigar into her direction with his mouth.

She reluctantly pulled out a lighter and ignited it below the end of the cigar.

"Thanks, dear." he said while winking at her and puffing out smoke into her direction.

Alexander and the CEO's eyes met once again.

"Please, tell me more, Dr. Lowe."

Hubert and Alexander looked at Lenny and the

airhostess in disapproval.

…

"Alright, alright… Sorry dear, we'll catch up later okay? Daddy's got some business to attend to." he said before slapping her backside crudely.

She quickly hurried off through the curtain.

"As it currently stands, Vettol provides cures for hundreds of ailments, correct?" asked Alexander.

"Correct."

"Every human being has a genetic makeup which is unique, even identical twins are not *exactly* the same. The differences can be vast or minor. These variances result in treatments that behave slightly differently, resulting in potential side effects."

"Dr. Lowe, this may come as a surprise to you, but I am not in the slightest bit interested in saving lives. I was told by Hubert that you could make us a lot of money. Please, get to the point!" he said, raising his voice.

Lenny nervously looked at Alexander, who was staring at the CEO cold faced, but undeterred.

"You *will* listen to me, you *will* appreciate the science behind this and most importantly, you *will* become significantly richer once this is in your hands.

Understood?"

The CEO stared back uncomfortably. It was clear that not many people had spoken to him like this before.

"Please proceed," said the greedy CEO.

"I am proposing that you no longer manufacture those treatments and-"

The CEO looked at Hubert with a confused look on his face.

"... and instead, you mass produce nanobots that can be programmed to cure the patient. There will no longer be any side effects, and every treatment will be bespoke to the individual."

The CEO began looking around frustrated, pulling himself up out of his slouching position.

"I don't understand a fucking word you're saying to me right now, talk normal! Talk money!" said the red faced CEO, nearly out of breath.

Hubert quickly began raising his hands in an automated gesture to defuse the sudden increase in tension. Alexander remained remarkably calm, his eyes caught Hubert's and he smiled before turning back to the CEO.

"Mr. Dean. That giant pile of money you are accumulating won't be of much use to you when you are ***dead***. Looking at your condition, your breathing, those sore spots on your body that you conceal, I would give you three years, five at a push."

"How fucking dare you!" shouted the CEO as struggled to hit feet out of his seat, he turned to Hubert "This is a waste of time! I didn't come here to be insulted and made to look a fool!"

"What if I told you that you could eat anything without gaining weight? What if I told you that I could remove the cholesterol currently caking the walls of your arteries within minutes? What if I told you that you are looking at the only person on this planet that could give you the cure to death, and grant you eternal life."

The CEO's focus and demeanour quickly changed.

"Eternal life? Live forever?"

Alexander nodded.

"This is a joke, right?" he said, looking at Hubert who shook his head.

"*I* am serious. Death is a disease, everyone on this planet, besides myself is slowly dying. There is no reason that *my* nanobots could not maintain your body long term."

The CEO pondered for a few moments, thinking through how this could be presented to his board of directors.

"Or…" said the CEO, pausing mid-thought "Short term. Our customers could pay a yearly subscription to maintain or replace these robots…"

Alexander's facial expression didn't change, but internally he was disgusted with the sack of meat slouching in the chair in front of him. He knew he had to keep calm and collected when it came to those surrounding Silver.

"Your genius knows no bounds, Mr. Dean." laughed Hubert, buttering up the CEO.

"So we'd throw away our existing products, saving us a fortune. Then adopt these robots, which can be told to cure anything?" asked the CEO as the jet began to move down the tarmac.

"Precisely."

"Imagine the worldwide media coverage! The clicks! How long would it take you to start this up?" asked the CEO eagerly.

"It's already been developed and it's ready for mass production." said Hubert equally as eager. "All the society asks for in return is 1% of Vettol's shares."

The figure did not phase the CEO who was still thinking through the enormous potential.

"So, IF you can make this happen…" said the CEO.

"There are no *ifs*, Mr. Dean. Only **when**." interrupted Alexander, to the displeasure of Hubert who sensed they were close to a deal.

"**IF**… you make this happen" reaffirmed the CEO with suspicion "Then you'd have a deal, provided that everything you've told me is accurate."

Hubert and Mr. Dean shook hands firmly as the plane began to speed down the runway before flying high into the sky.

Deep within the subconscious, the boy suddenly became alert. Time began to slow down significantly to match the flow of the outside world. Individual grains of sand could be seen hanging in the air.

"They just took off." said the boy as he kicked the football towards Alexander, who was standing between two pillars like a goalie.

"Looks like playtime is over unfortunately, Alex." said Alexander as he picked up the ball and walked over to him.

The boy nodded with a sad but accepting expression on his face.

"You know, Alexander, this time together has been so much fun. You're kinda like the big brother I always wanted."

"I thought you said I was a selfish lunatic?" quipped Alexander.

"Yeah you are, but I think it's okay for brothers to feel that way about each other, right?" joked the boy as he snatched the ball from Alexander playfully.

They both laughed. Alexander patted the boy's head similarly to how their mother did in a comforting gesture.

"You're a good boy, Alex. You've made all of this possible."

"Nah, teamwork!" said the boy enthusiastically.

"Alright, teamwork." admitted Alexander "We don't have much time though, unfortunately. Do you know what you need to do?"

"Yep, you can leave it all to me. I'll pass the messages on as best as I can."

To the boy's surprise, Alexander kneeled down and hugged the boy tightly. The white wisps moved between them. They began to whisper, letting out the same harmony as before, but it was much clearer.

…

"I can hear them clearly now, Alex." said Alexander as he was hugging his inner child. "This is… the lullaby that Mum used to sing to us when we were little."

The boy looked up in awe at the wisps over Alexander's shoulder, realising he was right, internally questioning what they might be.

"It is… isn't it? How could I forget…"

"Mum was always **very** proud of you."

Tears began to flow down the child's cheeks as the darkness enveloping him began to crack, slowly revealing the skin hiding beneath.

"Looks like we're both ready to move on now." said Alexander, letting go of his younger self.

The boy looked over his body in surprise, which was no longer shrouded in darkness, a sight he hadn't seen since before he entered this world.

"**Wow...** It's been a while..." said the boy with wonder.

"Sorry Alex, but we must begin... I wish we had more time."

"It's okay, I know how important the timings are..." said Alex, looking up to Alexander. "I'll miss ya, big bro..."

"I'll miss you too." said Alexander sombrely.

The boy began to quickly exit through the temple. As he was about to vanish out of sight, he slowed down. He looked back with doubt, like a child going to primary school for the first time.

"You got this." encouraged Alexander.

The boy smiled as fond memories of his school days played in his mind. He raised his hand to say goodbye.

"Good luck, little me." said Alexander under his breath as the boy vanished out of view for the last time.

"Here we go…"

In the outside world, they were now halfway over the Atlantic ocean. Alexander watched on as Hubert spoke with Mr. Dean. Lenny was still trying to flirt with the airhostess, who was clearly still very uncomfortable. He chuckled and looked out of the window, thinking through their next possible assignment. Suddenly, he felt a great pain behind his right eye, he sat forwards and exhaled deeply in agony.

"You alright, Champ?" asked Lenny, showing concern but keeping his hands firmly on the hips of the airhostess.

"Y-yes, It is prob-" but before he could respond fully, the pain became significantly stronger, causing him to scream out loud to the horror of those surrounding him.

"Get him some water, and tell the pilot to land urgently." said Lenny to the airhostess who quickly rushed away.

"You PESTS, what are you doing in there…" said Alexander to himself under his breath, grunting with a more sinister tone to his voice which Lenny had heard before.

Alexander was now bright red, with veins bulging out of his head. Hubert looked at Lenny with serious concern as he sat up in his chair.

"Has he done anything like this before?" asked Hubert.

"No, not at all, this is new." said a slightly panicked Lenny, which only served to worry Hubert more.

"Land the plane somewhere right now!" shouted Hubert towards the direction of the cockpit.

"*No.* Do not worry about *me*. I can handle this. I simply require sleep." said Alexander with a growl to his voice.

Lenny's demeanour immediately changed when Alexander uttered the word 'sleep'. He quickly jumped out of his seat.

"Do you need me to strap you down?" asked Lenny.

"No, he is not a fool. He will not come back, he is likely just acting up. I will make this *very* quick." replied Alexander.

"What's his deal?" asked the CEO to Hubert in confusion.

"Nothing, he'll be fine. He's had some very bad experiences when it comes to flying." assured Hubert.

Alexander sat back in his chair, overcome with pain and forced his body into a sudden deep sleep.

In the subconscious, the white cracks returned and burst

open suddenly out of nowhere in all directions. These cracks were much larger than they had ever been before. This pushed the dark clouds far away into the distance and kicked up a lot of sand into the air, leaving only a haunting orange cracked sky once the sand settled back onto the surface. Alexander materialised from the outside world into the red desert. He looked behind himself and noticed the temple that was towering over him.

"This fucking place, ***again?!***" he shouted angrily.

He quickly made his way into the temple and saw Alexander, sitting down on the floor staring at him with a confident smile on his face. He was confronted with himself once again, two Alexander's, two very different personalities.

"What do you think ***you*** are doing?!" shouted Alexander while pacing forwards.

Alexander, who was still sitting on the floor of the temple, placed both of his palms on the ground below him.

"I was hoping we'd meet again."

"***I*** am amazed, truly. I guess my last warning was not clear enough, ***was it***? Do you not care about that boy's wellbeing, or even your own? Do I have to punish you both another way? Trust me when I say, ***THAT*** was nothing compared to what ***I*** am truly capable of!" shouted Alexander scathingly.

Alexander did not answer, and remained still on the floor, focusing on the ground below him.

"This fucking temple..." he gestured to the hand carved walls "That childish apparition keeps finding a way to rebuilt it. I swear I will find a way to smother that brat once and for all now that I have primary control." said Alexander, as a slight rumble could be felt all around them.

Parts of the temple began to fall down, to the surprise of his alter ego.

...

He finally noticed Alexander's appearance.

"*Wait...*" he said, analysing his alter ego. "*Why... how* are you no longer shrouded in darkness?" asked Alexander, suddenly far more alert to his surroundings "What is happening here?"

Alexander smiled at his alter ego.

"*Where...* is that child?"

Alexander awoke. He breathed in deeply as if his lungs had no oxygen in them. Red sand fell around him onto the seats and floor of the private jet.

"What the fuck?!" shouted Hubert, quickly unbuckling his seatbelt and standing himself up away from the sand. The CEO did the same and they hurried over to the other side of the jet.

Alexander shielded his eyes, overwhelmed with the amount of detail in this world. He squinted and began to look around in awe and wonder at his surroundings, then down at his larger body. The pain to his senses was intense, but it was quickly put aside when he noticed the football in his hands which he had brought from the subconscious.

"W-" he realised he couldn't speak very well, but managed to push through it "W-woah…" he said, standing up for a moment in excitement to see how tall he was before quickly sitting back down, examining his hands and the football closely.

"You… you doing okay over there, Champ?" asked Lenny, who was also slowly unbuckling his seatbelt. He carefully leaned forward to Alexander cautiously.

Alexander ignored him and looked outside the window, finding himself surrounded by a seemingly endless blue world. His eyes welled with tears.

"*Soooooo* cool…" said Alexander under his breath "It's *SO* blue! Just like I remembered…" he said, looking over to the maroon suited man happily, before quickly realising who he was.

"L-Lenny?! No way. Is that really you?!" asked Alexander in a more joyful and surprised tone "You look so old now!" he laughed.

"Hey!" shouted Hubert to Alexander who had to cover his ears in pain "What is happening, answer me right now!"

"Alexander, is that you?" asked Lenny, trying to control the conversation. He carefully stood himself up and clenched his fists.

Alexander's awe turned to a more neutral expression as he moved his hands back to the football.

...

"You guys are right to be afraid of me…" he said softly with some sadness behind his voice.

Hubert pulled out a gun to the surprise of the CEO who let out a small yelp.

"Don't even think about it, Hubert." instructed Lenny uncharacteristically to his superior.

"Who is *he*?" asked Hubert to Lenny, but he made no response, his full focus was on Alexander.

Alexander looked around the room, looking at everyone individually, including the airhostess who had just entered the room after hearing the commotion.

"Sorry… we didn't mean for you guys to be caught up in our mess. Especially you, Lenny…" said Alexander regretfully.

Something deep within Lenny felt excited to see this version of Alexander, as if something was wanting to escape and reach out to him. He looked down at the football, recognising it from their childhood, it was the one they stole from a bully at school who used to pick on Alexander until Lenny stepped in. He quickly suppressed those thoughts and feelings, focusing instead on the more important matter at hand. Alexander moved his gaze back to the window, trying to remember the lines that were fed to him before he woke up.

"The average human being weighs… around eighty kilograms? Oh wait, I think he said seventy? There's around SEVEN OCTILLION atoms in the human body… that's a seven followed by… twenty seven zeros? I think it was, anyway, it's a **really** big number! It would take twice the length of the universe to count to that if you started now. Do you know what would happen if you converted all of those atoms into energy?"

Nobody answered.

"An explosion of that magnitude would be around 1.5 megatons of TNT. A weapon of impeccable destruction!" said Alexander, impressed with himself for remembering all of those words and numbers.

Within the subconscious, Alexander's palms began to glow, which spread outwards across the desert and sky in all directions.

"*EXPLAIN!*" roared Alexander.

"You left us no choice, other than total annihilation. You will pay dearly for what you did to Mary, to Steven, his family, colleagues... and to us," said Alexander in disgust.

"*No...* you... ***please! DO NOT DO THIS! YOU WILL KILL US BOTH!***" screamed Alexander as he began to rush forwards.

"Good."

"*NO!*" shouted Alexander within arms reach of his alter ego.

"Goodbye... *'Primary'*..." said Alexander to himself with a regretful tear in his eye.

Everything around them immediately filled with a blinding white light, as if they were in the centre of a star.

In the outside world, Alexander's body began to glow to the horror of everyone onboard. Within a split second, everything around them turned into a white hot fireball with temperatures in the hundreds of millions of degrees. The blast erupted into the blue sky above, quickly turning into a mushroom cloud in the middle of the Atlantic Ocean as everything around them was annihilated into nothingness…

XV

"Earlier today at precisely 07:08 UTC, a powerful blast was observed over the Atlantic Ocean. So far nobody has claimed responsibility for the incident and there hasn't been any reported casualties. No nuclear fallout had been observed, leading to speculation on the cause. Scientists are theorising that it might have been a previously unobserved comet, similar to the Tunguska event in 1908 over Russia which caused a similar explosion. The blast produced a brief flash that was witnessed by many in the Americas and Europe for a few seconds. We'll update you once we have more information. Bradley Ryker, BBC News."

The following year, Dr. Woodfine continued on the legacy of Dr. Steven Abel and his team, publicly announcing the nanobot technology to the world. He had patented and licensed the technology to very specific non-profit and public health organisations around the world, ensuring that private organisations could not profit from it.

...

XV

Deep within an otherworldly place, Alexander awoke. The light was gleaming off every reflective surface of the room, illuminating it. The white light was overwhelming, but it was very comforting. As it dissipated slightly, he looked at the clock, which showed **08:08**. Still dazed, he moved his hand towards the other side of the large bed. As he did so, Mary cuddled up next to him, rubbing his arm comfortingly.

"Good morning, Allie." she said with a hopeful smile.

"Good morning, my lovely…"

Acknowledgements

A massive thank you to my beta readers Alice, Jeroen, Jess and Lindy who gave me very honest and valuable feedback over the years which helped refine the story.

Tom J Davis is an incredible artist and one of my closest friends. He spent a very long time working on the cover for the novel and I can't thank him enough for what he did. It's perfect!

Thank you to all of my family and friends who encouraged and supported me over the last 12ish years while writing *Door 808*. You're the best.

And most of all, my beautiful wife, Lindy, who has been my biggest supporter throughout this wild journey, giving me the motivation I needed. She even made the Silver vulture pin which you can see on the right! Thank you for everything, my lovely.

What's next?

The world of *Door 808* will return in a prequel which delves into Alexander's rough upbringing, his friendship with Lenny and the inner workings of the secret society known simply as Silver.

Door808.com

Reading Group Questions

1. Were there moments when you found yourself siding with the more sadistic Alexander, even if briefly?
2. Which other character do you feel had the most potential if given more focus, and why?
3. The red desert is a constant throughout the story. How did you visualise it, and what do you think it symbolised?
4. In what ways does grief shape Alexander's choices? Did this affect your sympathy for him?
5. What events from Alexander's upbringing do you think turned him into the person he became?
6. Were there particular scenes or lines that stuck with you after finishing *Door 808*?
7. What emotions did the story leave you with?

Feedback

If you have <u>any</u> feedback on *Door 808*, I'd **love** to hear it. You can email me at <u>SiLinkBooks@gmail.com</u> or feel free to leave a review wherever you picked up the book / eBook.

Thank you again for your support.

www.ingramcontent.com/pod-product-compliance
Ingram Content Group UK Ltd.
Pitfield, Milton Keynes, MK11 3LW, UK
UKHW042210171025
464044UK00001B/8